Predator

Corinne Miller

Contents

Prologue

I t was cold.

That was her first thought as she stepped off the tiny little plane and onto Russian territory. Even after being in New York for almost four years, this was still a new feeling to her. This was a new kind of cold; the kind that stings your skin each time the wind blows and turns you blue and pink. She still shivered beneath her layers of thick coats and scarves that covered her body.

Upon exiting the plane, she found a short, balding man with plump, rosy cheeks holding a sign that read her name. Struggling with her many bags, she waddled over to him and smiled.

"Hi, I'm Grey."

He frowned and looked down at the sign before smiling widely. "Oh! Miss Clarke!" Her name sounded weird on his foreign tongue. "Yes, come. You need help?"

"Please." She gave a small smile and he gave a chortle before grabbing a few bags from her hands and leading her to his little cab.

Once all the bags were in the trunk except for one that hung off Grey's shoulder constantly, she climbed inside the warm vehicle and the man began to drive.

She leaned over, peering out the window at the land around her. White mountains lined the dark gray sky, snow covered the every inch of everything in thick layers and there were forests all around her it seemed. She could feel the silence through the window as she stared at the snow-capped canopies and sighed as the warm feeling of peace flooded her veins.

"You like Russia?" The driver spoke with a eager nod and smile.

"It's quite beautiful. Have you always lived here?"

"I born in St. Petersburg, few miles South of here. I move here at twenty-nine and stay." His English was choppy but she didn't mind as he seemed to be thrilled to be talking to her about his country. "Russia is home."

Grey smiled softly as she leaned back in the seat and watched the snowy land pass by outside. Besides the trees, it seemed there was nothing but nature and life blooming through snow that creatures pranced over. It was breathtaking.

Soon it seemed that the many trees got thinner and in their place grew little homes that puffed smoke from their chimneys in hopes of warming the bodies inside. There were few people outdoors at this time. Bundled in thick fur-lined coats, carrying stacks of wood in their gloved hands, each breath fanning into the air before them. They were men usually, hauling wood back to their families or large axes rested on their shoulders as they walked towards the forest. She saw only a couple women who merely stood outside to greet their returning husband before ushering him into the warm home.

Further down the long, winding road, a town formed. The cab driver drove to the center, where little shoppes and stores lined the brick road that branched off into few roads that more cabin-like homes surrounded and even one road that was barely hidden by the snow leading to the forest.

Grey swiftly climbed out after the driver who scurried to open the trunk for her and set her bags on the cold ground.

"How much do I owe you?"

The man gave her a price and she obliged, placing the money in his open palm.

"Sir, do you mind if I take a picture of you and your cab?" Grey asked slowly, so he could clearly understand her and his eyes light up and he nodded.

The man hurried over to the side of his cab and placed an arm on top and smiled the moment Grey pulled out her camera. After snapping a photo, he asked to see it.

"I look good!" He smiled. "This go in American magazine?"

"I do quite hope so." She replied which only caused him to smile more.

His hand buried in his pocket and he pulled out the rubles she had given him earlier and placed them back in her hand. "I need no money if you put me in magazine." He said. "Thank you."

"What's your name?"

"Klaus."

"I'll see to it that you get a copy of the magazine when it's printed."

"It was pleasure to meet you, Miss Clarke."

Grey gave him a smile and a sheepish wave as he drove away, leaving her alone in an unfamiliar town where she had no doubt no one spoke a lick of English. He had dropped her off in front of a little road that had few houses, one of which being hers for the next few months. She remembered her boss had showed her a picture of her new home, a cabin basically that only differed from the others around it because it was uninhabited.

She strolled down the road, lugging her bags on her shoulders or rolling over the cold snow, in search of her home. Finding the only house that wasn't puffing out smoke with dark windows was simple and she was thankful since her arms were already beginning to ache. Stumbling into the cold cabin, she dropped her bags and huffed, making her way to the first candle she saw and lighting it with the matches that had been laying beside it. It's flame illuminated the cabin in a dim orange glow

She could now make out the rooms and furniture that littered her home. The room she stood in was a living room with nothing but a bookshelf with dusty books lining it's shelves and a old couch in front of a fireplace and coffee table. On the other side of the room was the kitchen which consisted of a few counters and a stove and a fridge that looked older than her, and a tiny little table with one chair against a wall. There were two doors; one to a bathroom that when she walked in, she was hissed at by a furry rat who scurried past her feet making her squeal. The other door lead to where she'd be sleeping on a old bed that looked ready to break and a small dresser across from it, other than that a simple night table and a rug adorned the room.

With a sigh she moved back to her bags and began to haul them to her new room.

"Home sweet home." She muttered.

Part One

{ picture - marloes horst as grey}

The shutter made a ticking noise as it captured multiple frames of the deer leaping over the snow bank. She pulled the camera from her face, her own breath fogging the air as she watched the animal disappear beneath the falling snow.

It seemed endless, the snow. It had been falling all last night and through-out most of today and it amazed her. She sunk in the snow with each step and if she stood still she had no doubt the snow would reach above her knees. She didn't mind one bit though. She lived for weather like this.

With a pink nose and cheeks to match, she moved through the snow and closer to the forest in hopes of getting more than just a deer leaping through a winter wonderland. She'd heard some of the English speaking natives that morning as she walked to the forest, speaking about a recent wolf attack a few towns over. She wasn't worried; the closest town was miles away.

As she got deeper into the forest, she found the snow untouched only tainted by a few large paw prints that stir uneasiness in the pit of her stomach. She crouched down, taking a few shots of snow-capped ivy that weaved up the trees. As she stood again, she found herself no longer alone, another presence causing hairs on the back of her neck to rise beneath her scarf.

Through the trees she could make out a pack of them running through the forest. Their panting filled the once quiet area along with the sound of pure snow crunching beneath their weight. As she pulled the camera to her face and begin to take pictures, her presence didn't go as unnoticed as she thought. One wolf's head turning and locking eyes with her through the camera lens as it ran. It's gaze sent a shiver down her back and after capturing a few more shots, she quickly turned and scurried out of the forest and away from possible danger.

•

It seemed as if the town gave her the creeps more than wolves in a forest did. Grey sat in the corner of a little diner and she could feel the townspeople's stares as she sipped her coffee. She ignored their gazes and set her own on the screen of her camera as she flicked through the photos she took that morning. They were breathtaking, the photos, and she was extremely proud to go back to America and show her boss what she's done.

Taking another long sip of her coffee, she studied another photo of the wolves running by. Zooming in she could see each muscle defined beneath their fur as they were frozen in mid-run, every hair and every scar that marred their skin. One photo she had she could even see the wolf's eyes, a bright shade of a copper color against it's gray fur. A frown took place on her face as she zoomed in on another photo, looking closer at what was taking place in the background.

She almost choked on her coffee at what was hidden in her picture. Behind all the wolves, further into the trees, was a man - if she could call it that. This man was hardly even a man in her photo. He was hunched over, his back to her, the skin there having ripped open to show bloody red muscle and in some spots, what looked like fur sprouting out. She could see a few of his bones sticking out of place and what looked like claws growing from his fingers that tore at the skin of his back.

Her breathing had become shaky and a light sheet of sweat had made her skin look pale and gray. Slowly setting down her camera, she put her elbows on the table and ran her hands down her face repeatedly as she kept glancing back at the photo. There was nothing in her head that made sense of this photo. Nothing that could've explained what she was looking at. Her mind was reeling from the revelation that this couldn't have been her imagination because she had it on film.

Grey felt sick as she studied the photo closer, looking at the man

•

She scanned the final page of the book once again, not ready to admit she still was clueless as to what was in that picture. She'd read countless of books she found at the little library, none of which had anything that lead her to believe what she's been looking at is true. But it had to be; she'd been staring at the picture for the last three and a half hours trying to figure out if the image had somehow been distorted or something but there were no logical answers. She'd gone through countless books on anthropology and biology but there was still nothing that settled that feeling in the pit of her stomach.

Running her fingers through her hair, Grey released a sigh as she closed yet another book. Leaning back against the couch she threw it onto the coffee table and it slid off with a thunk.

"God-"

Grey frowned, looking at a book she hadn't even seen before that was now visible thanks to the book that was on the floor. Picking it up she wiped the layer of dust that hid the cover with a disgusted face that quickly vanished when she saw the title and the image on the cover.

She whispered the title as if it was a sin to speak the word. "Lycanthropy."

A cold shudder slithered down her spine as her eyes left the ancient looking words to stare at the image beneath them. The image that had been carved into the book was oddly familiar to Grey and that scared her. For on the cover of that book was a drawing of a man, standing tall, proud and bare, with the head of a wolf bearing razor sharp teeth.

"This is impossible. . ." She tried to convince herself once again that she was going insane but the crack of thunder outside wasn't what made her skin crawl. It was the deep howl that followed shortly after that made her question her sanity as she opened the book.

Part Two

Grey had been in that cabin for two days, reading and rereading the book on lycanthropy as much as she could, thanks to the countless amounts of google translate from her phone. She finally left the safety of her temporary home to go get something to eat at the diner, the book still in her hand along with a new one she'd picked up on the way there. At the diner, she found a lonely little booth back in the corner, still not hidden from the curious eyes of the locals. Her nose was buried in the book as she sat against a window, sipping on her coffee and occasionally nibbling on the pastry on her plate.

"Lycanthropy?" A voice spoke across from her, causing Grey to squeak and drop her book. It bounced off the table and into her lap with a thud, barely missing her coffee. Thank god the coffee survived. She looked up at the girl with wide eyes who smirked. "Interesting choice for a girl like you."

"Excuse you?" Grey glared at the girl now sat across from her as she squeezed the book tight against her legs.

"That's a dangerous subject, girl." The girl's slender fingers started to reach for the pastry Grey had been nibbling on and she slapped her hand away. She arched a brow at her actions, that smirk still on her face. "If you're not careful it'll take you somewhere you don't want to go."

"It's not real." Grey stated, not sure if she was trying to convince herself or this odd girl.

The girl shrugged and they fell into a silence as her big eyes looked out the window. She changed the topic. "Everyone's talking about you, you know?"

"What?" She frowned and she slowly grabbed the book from her lap and closed it, setting it on the table. The girls eyes found it.

She hummed. "A new girl comes to town, pretty face, long legs, gorgeous eyes, everyone already talks about the very - and I mean very - few tourists our town gets but when someone who actually doesn't look like a ved'ma comes in, we'll definitely talk."

"Look like a what?"

She kept talking. "I mean, especially with that fancy camera that had to cost more than every belonging in this town. And then, you were carrying it through the forest - which, might I warn you, is very stupid of you." The girl rambled on, leaving Grey absolutely confused. "But honestly you're not like the other tourists I've seen. You're different. You don't try to explore the town and instead explore the trees, and you don't talk to any of the natives."

"I didn't think anyone knew English. . ."

"The elders don't, but some of the younger generation is forced to learn it." The girl shrugged and flicked her yellow hair over her shoulder. "I'm Petra by the way."

"Grey."

She scanned her up and down before quirking an eyebrow. "Suits you."

Grey frowned and moved her tongue to press against the side of her mouth with a scoff like noise. But she ignored her comment, mind still on her past words. "Wait, why was going into the forest stupid?" She wasn't dumb, she knew it was idiotic to return to those trees but she thought maybe this girl had the answer to her questions.

Petra leaned back in the seat, arms folding as she perked up a single brow at Grey - that seemed to be her look. "When I was little, my grandmother used to tell me bedtime stories about this forest. There were so many different ones, I've lost track. About the trees, the original wolves, all that lovely stuff, but the one that every single elder has told each new generation was the one about the khishchnik , the predator. It scared every one of us when we were little, it was a legend of course but we were naive. It made me fear the forest."

"What was it about?"

Petra's brow ticked up and a smirk took place upon her lips as she shrugged. "I couldn't tell 'ya. You see, I don't remember it; I haven't heard it since I was little."

"Oh."

"But. . ." She leaned forward, too close for Grey's liking and smiled so that her sharp incisors were on display. Those aren't normal. "I'm sure my grandmother would gladly tell you if you're interested." Grey perked up at her words.

"Would she really?"

"Tomorrow night come to my house and I'll get her to tell you." Said Petra. "Go down the west road, last house on the left."

And with that, Petra stood and she began to walk out, but not before leaving Grey with parting words.

"If I were you Grey, I'd stay far away from the forest and it's stories. See you tomorrow."

And she was walking away with one last smirk sent Grey's way, who was left at the booth absolutely stunned at that girl and if it wasn't for the feeling deep in her gut, she would've forgotten those directions to the yellow-haired girl's home but it seemed her mind wouldn't erase it no matter how hard she tried.

With a shake of her head, Grey grabbed her books, put some money of the table and left the diner; Petra nowhere in sight.

• • •

That night, the howls returned with blankets of falling snow. Outside, a blizzard raged through northern Russia and inside, Grey was huddling beneath layers upon layers of blankets in front of a fire, trying to keep her body from shivering.

The book was gripped tight beneath her pink fingers, shaking ever so slightly as she tried to read the pages. The further into the book on lycanthropy she got, the more everything seemed to click yet fall out of place. What she'd seen in the forest was called a "lycan" which was a mystical being that was not supposed to exist but she - of all people - had proof of it on camera. Stories in the book told the species was very secluded, they kept to their own kind and didn't dare to venture too close to human, fearing the risk of exposure; for if they were exposed, Grey had no doubt the government would be capturing them for testing and people would be hunting them down.

The more she read, the more she felt as if the world she'd grown up and had learned to live in was slowly fading away and being replaced by this new world full of things she didn't even know about. She felt as if she was in the dark her entire life and now it seemed as if every past memory was just a dream and this was the harsh reality of life. Nothing was real anymore but that which was told to be mythical. It couldn't be real; but no matter what she told herself, she knew it was true.

Groaning she closed the book and ran her fingers through her tangled hair. Grey felt like she was going insane - no she was going insane. Believing in fairytales and bedtime stories. Searching for proof of a man who could take the shape of a wolf. Finding truths in what she had always been told were make believe. She felt like she couldn't breathe. Grey quickly stood to her feet, scurrying to her room where she changed into warmer clothes and slid on sturdy boots and a thick coat before she stuffed all her hair into up and underneath a beanie. With a flashlight and her camera in hand, she opened the front door and walked directly into the storm.

• • •

The wind was brutal as it whipped around, sending little shards of ice pelting against Grey's exposed skin. Despite all her layers of clothing, the cold still found its way to her skin and caused her body to shiver. The flashlight in her hands did little to create a view through the viciously falling snow and it only seemed to make her surroundings harder to see. She stopped moving, not knowing where she was in the forest yet again and leaned against a thick tree. After a moment of catching her breath and calling herself stupid, she decided to reach for her camera in hopes that maybe she'd capture something in this storm on that.

Grey took a few photos of her surroundings but found nothing as she looked around and with a sigh she continued trekking deeper into forest until the only sound was that of the howling wind and the snow crunching beneath her weight. Pausing again, she watched as the wind slowed down the slightest and the thick snowflakes became little specs of ice falling from the thick treetops that provided a canopy to shelter her from the storm. While she could still hear the wind howling from a distance, it's violent breeze didn't reach how far she was in the forest. At this point, deep in the trees, the world seemed almost magical.

A chill ran down Grey's spine and she shuddered beneath her layers of clothes. The hair on the back of her neck rose to attention and she hesitantly reached for her camera and pulled it up to her face. Unable to see anything she flicked up the flash and clicked, the light from the camera illuminating the forest around her. A shadow appeared between two trees and Grey gasped. She stumbled back as the shadow sauntered forward and a growl echoed through the trees.

What left Grey's lips could be considered somewhat of a terrified shriek as she tripped over her own feet and found herself buried beneath snow. The shadowed creature's snort was muffled by all the snow covering Grey, which she was quickly digging through. When she resurfaced, her beanie had come off and her hair was a wild mess dotted with delicate snowflakes, her eyes wide as she looked at the creature that was now visible under the tiniest bit of moonlight that peeked through the thick leaves.

With its lip pulled back to reveal sharp canines dripping with saliva, it took a step forward once more, muscles rippling beneath it's auburn fur. The wolf was massive, legs long and thick like it's body, with huge paws that showed off its sharp claws. It's ears were drawn back to it's head and calculating eyes were on her; the prey.

This wolf was the predator and she was merely it's helpless, weak prey that stood no chance against it's large, razor sharp teeth.

It began to take another step but froze, ears perked up as it's head tilted to the side curiously. The snarl was lost and the growling subsided to what sounded like a little whine. It's eyes were a shimmering blue, watching Grey. Then, all of the sudden, the wolf was gone and Grey was left shivering in the snow.

{fun question: How old do y'all think I am?? M xx}

Part Three

{ picture above - Petra's home}

The walkway to Petra's home seemed endless to Grey as she approached the large cabin, to each side of her the snow was piled up in high walls where they had pushed the fallen snow from the walkway. Her hands shook tucked in the pockets of her coat, her fingers subconsciously running over the glossy pictures stuffed in her pocket, no doubt leaving it tainted with her smudged fingerprints. Her fingers had to momentarily leave the warmth of her pockets to push open the white gate in front of the home, that seemed to practically blend in with the snowy surroundings. She closed it behind her carefully and walked up the steps.

Slowly raising her hand, she knocked on the door and not a moment later, Petra stood in the doorway with her signature smirk.

"Grey!" She exclaimed, leaning against the doorframe. "I was beginning to think you'd never show up."

"Here I am." Grey shrugged. "I-uh-I have something I need to show you."

"Later? My grandmother is anxious to meet you! Come in!"

Petra pulled Grey inside the house and draped a skinny arm over her shoulder, which proved to be kind of hard seeing as Grey was a solid few inches taller than the petite girl. She still continued leading her into the kitchen where heavenly smells floated in the air, originating from food Grey was not familiar with. Stood in front of the stove, was a small woman with hair the color of the moon that flowed down to her hips in thick waves with thin, pale arms that whisked whatever was was cooking in the pan.

"Babushka eto Grey." Petra murmured softly into the woman's ear, her hand on her shoulder gently.

The old woman set down her cooking utensils and wiped her arms down her apron before turning then, her dark eyes finding Grey's and narrowing in on her. Her eyes were beady and harsh as they scanned Grey up and down, a brow arching up as her lips pushed out in a purse.

"Grey, this is my grandmother."

Grey looked at the woman with a small smile. "It's nice to meet you."

"Eto smertnyy?" The woman turned to Petra with a very obvious sneer that she didn't bother to hide.

"Babushka!"

"It nice to meet you, child." The woman nodded at Grey before turning back to her food. "Dinner ready soon. Petra, get little ones."

"Be right back." Petra gave Grey a small smile before moving to the stairs and climbing them. Grey watched Petra as she stood at the top and yelled out: "Grandmother's made dinner! Come get it or get your ass whooped!"

"These are your little siblings?" Grey laughed from the bottom and Petra's eyes as well as her grandmother's found Grey.

"Technically yes, but they're more or less like little demons."

All doors on the second floor seemed to open at once and one older boy and a smaller boy followed by an even littler girl behind them. They all scrambled past the girl and down the stairs where not one took notice of Grey due to their grandmother scolding them in her rough Russian tongue.

When Petra too descended the stairs, she looked to Grey and smirked. "After dinner, my grandmother will tell you aboutkhishchnik. Come, her cooking is the best in town."

Petra lead Grey to the dining room where an older boy was helping the old woman place food at each seat. Grey was shown to her seat, right in the middle of the table beside Petra.

"Who are you?" A delicate voice spoke from beside Grey and her eyes found a small brown haired girl standing beside her chair, her front teeth missing and her fingers wrapped around a delicate teddy bear.

"Rosalie." Petra snapped and the little girl scurried to her own seat. "Eat grandmother's food. Don't let it go to waste."

"I was just-"

"That is Grey. She's new here and my new friend so no being obnoxious little brats, yes?"

"I'm Dimitri." The older boy was now sat at the end of the table and gave smile to Grey. He looked no older than sixteen and seemed to be the oldest besides Petra.

"That's Ethen, he's the quietest and least evil out of our bunch."

The little boy stared at Grey with wide green eyes, innocence filled the air around him and she couldn't help but find him adorable with those doe eyes and messy chocolate hair. She gave him a smile which he did not return, he just kept staring at her.

"Why are you here?" Rosalie asked through a mouthful of food. Petra scolded her behavior and she quickly swallowed and asked the question again.

"Your grandmother is going to tell me a story later."

"What story?" Dimitri smirked as he leaned back the slightest in his chair.

"Khishchnik."

His relaxed behavior was gone and now he sat straight up in his seat with tense shoulders. "That's a brave choice." His voice was gruff and he quickly looked down at his food.

"That story is scary why do you want to hear it?" Rosalie's shaky voice brought Grey's curious eyes away from Dimitri.

"I'm sort of writing a story of my own and that legend is going to help me a lot." Grey smiled sweetly at the little girl.

The old woman beside her scoffed. "Khishchnik is no legend."

"I thought-"

"Where are you from?" Rosalie spoke up again, with wide eyes. "What kind of story are you writing?"

"I live in the United States, New York." The girls big eyes twinkled with amazement. "I came here to take pictures of the animals and land here, and I'll write about my experience once I return home."

"Does Babushka's story have to do with your stuff?"

"Well, it wasn't supposed to but-"

Petra interrupted, clapping her hands together. "Alright, little ones, bedtime. Go on! Dimitri, can you take care of the dishes while I tend to Babushka and our guest?"

The boy nodded and quickly gathered the plates as Petra helped her grandmother to the couch in the living room by the fire, Grey following behind. Rosalie and Ethen carefully walking up the stairs to disappear into their own rooms.

Once the group settled in silence in the living room, the old woman raised a brow and looked at Grey.

"Before I tell you story, I ask why you want to hear tale of khishchnik?"

She bit her lip, fingers going to the pictures in her pocket before retreating. "I believe I've seen this beast you speak of."

The woman scoffed. "No one who sees khishchnik lives. He is beast. He kill for pleasure. Nikto ne zhivet, chtoby rasskazat' skazku."

"I swear ma'am. I-" Grey stumbled over her words as she reached in her pocket. "I have proof."

The old woman shakily took the photos and lifted them up, squinting her eyes at the first photo; one she took last night of that auburn wolf.

"This just common wo-"

Her voice was lost as she discarded the wolf picture to the one of the man, mid "shift", so it was called in the books. Her free hand came up to cover her mouth and she looked up at Grey with fearful eyes.

"Where did you get this?"

"I took it ma'am, a few days ago in the forest."

She shook her head as she stood and Petra took the photo, her brows furrowing together as she looked at the picture. Petra tensed when she saw it. The old woman began to walk out but she stopped and turned around slowly, dark eyes on Grey.

"You must leave."

"Wait, what? Why?"

"Now." The woman continued to babble words in Russian, her eyes closing as if she was praying.

Grey looked to Petra for answers but the girl was staring at the photo in awe and fear. "Petra?"

She looked up at her friend, eyes swirling with an emotion Grey had never seen before. She simply shook her head. "You need to leave."

"Petra-"

"Let's go. Now."

Once outside, Petra hurried off and Grey had to jog to keep up despite her height advantage. She was practically panting by the time she caught up to Petra and they stood by the empty barn, facing the forest. The girl stared out into the darkness of the forest as Grey leaned over to catch her breath.

"What happened in there?" Grey exclaimed, fuming, still breathing heavy either from running after Petra or anger - she couldn't tell.

Petra spun around, holding the picture up to Grey. "You saw this with your own eyes?" She nodded. "You swear?"

"I mean-I didn't see it I just took the picture and when I went to look through what I had he was there in the back and-"

"Grey." Grey's mouth snapped shut and she looked to Petra who was look-ing at the picture again. She muttered something in Russian and ran her hand through her hair before leaning against the rickety old barn. "That's why you were reading the books. It all makes sense. . . And then, you didn't listen to me and went back into the forest?!"

"I had to, Petra. I feel like I'm losing my mind."

Petra's hand ran through her own hair again as a sigh escaped her chapped lips. "Grey, there's a lot you don't know about this world-"

"What are you talking about?"

"-I don't know how to explain it all nicely without you freaking out and I don't want you to think I'm crazy because honestly, you're the only normal friend I have and I quite liked a bit of normalcy in my life."

"Petra, spit it out." Grey took a step back as Petra's expression changed dramatically.

From worried and scared, she went to terrifying with her eyes no longer a deep blue but a color that shined beneath the moonlight. A bright flame danced in her eyes and Grey stumbled back in shock, her hand covering her mouth. She stood before the human girl looking like a predator, staring down at her with inhumane eyes. Never before had Grey been so scared, not even around that wolf that had gotten so close to her. Her friend was not what she believed her to be, and that thought of reality slipping away beneath her fingertips was back and she was more scared than ever.

"You're not crazy. What you saw in the forest, Grey, that was a shifter or from what you've read, a lycan." Petra said carefully, assessing Grey's reaction before taking in a deep breath. "Grey, they're real. You have proof of our species."

"Our. . .?"

"My whole family and I are lycans."

{Translations:Babushka eto Grey.-Grandmother this is GreyEto smert-nyy?-Translates to: "Its mortal?" but in this case it's more like "this is the human?"Nikto ne zhivet, chtoby rasskazat' skazku.-no one lives to tell the tale}

Part Four

- -

{ picture - Grey's cabin}{WARNING: GRAPHIC CONTENT}

There comes a time in life, when one realizes that childhood has ended. Whatever causes this realization, that thing, that event is unforgettable and it looms in the back of one's head and causes a hatred to bloom for this one specific thing. A hatred forming for that one event, good or bad, that caused the sweet facade of life to fade away and in its place the ability to see life as it is. To accept that life is tough and that childhood was an intricately spun web of lies and details, all created in order to protect one from the harsh realities that is adulthood; this is an extremely hard thing to do but when it is accepted, everything isn't as bad anymore for some strange reason.

And Grey's first reaction to an end to childhood, was to cry, to deny everything she'd just been told and run. Run far away from this life and back to the one she lived before all this, where everything was normal and good. But there was something, something buried within the depths of her beating heart that told her to stay, and that something good had to come of all of this. So that was what lead Grey and Petra to the forest, where Grey stood shivering beneath the falling snow while Petra seemed perfectly fine as she stripped down to nothing but her skivvies.

Grey was shaking, not only from the freezing cold but from the fear that rattled her to the core of what was to come of this discovery. Her entire life had been a lie, all the bedtime stories had been true, there were creatures that shouldn't exist lurking around the world. These beasts were everywhere according to Petra. If it was possible, Grey felt further away from sanity than she did before and all that seemed to be missing now was a glass slipper or a talking teacup.

"Are you ready?" Petra's voice broke Grey's thoughts, soft and cautious, as if Grey would break with the wrong tone of voice.

Grey nodded, not trusting her voice and Petra gave the girl a weak smile before closing her eyes and sucking in a breath.

For a moment, there was silence in the forest that calmed Grey before it was broken by a guttural groan from Petra's throat along with a snap. Grey flinched. The girl's next scream and dislocation of a bone in her arm drowned out of the sound of Grey's phone ringing in her pocket, her eyes unable to leave Petra's form. She fell to the ground next, moaning in pain as sharp claws grew from her fingertips and she dug them into her own back, ripping the skin there to reveal bloodied blonde fur. The bones beneath Petra's patches of skin and fur could be seen moving, snapping and reshaping themselves into an entirely new being. Then the most gruesome thing seemed to happen; the finale.

Grey felt nauseous and lightheaded when Petra's eyes rolled out of her skull and fell to the ground, even more so when her jaw snapped and her teeth fell from her bloody gums. Out of her broken jaw, came a snout that was bearing it's sharp teeth in a growl, following that, came a head with eyes the color of a flame shining bright. Once the head was completely out of

Petra's body, it began to shake it own body, causing blood and skin and shards of bone to fly off her fur and into the air.

Then, the night became silent around them, the air cool as snow continued to flutter down from the sky. The white snowflakes surrounded two bodies and nipped at one's skin and settled in the other's fur. In front of Grey stood a beast in bloodied snow; a gigantic, blonde wolf that stared at her with it's head cocked to the side, it's tail and ears perked up in attention.

"P-Petra?"

The wolf chuffed at the sound of it's name and Grey laughed the slightest at the noise. A wave of dizziness hit her like a truck and she swayed on her feet, a twisting feel in her gut. Her eyes fluttered as she stared at the wolf and blinked again and again.

"I think I'm gonna be-"

Grey was cut off as her body hunched over and convulsed, the food from earlier staining the snow. She gagged and gasped as it came up again and she swayed on her feet, her legs shaking. Petra whined at the sight and trotted over to her, nudging her legs making Grey stumble and almost fall as her body heaved again, this time nothing coming up. The wolf nudging her whined louder this time and the heavy crunching of snow approached them.

"Petra?" Dimitri was then standing by them, frowning, his face showing his shock openly. "What's going on?"

She made a noise at the back of her throat like a groan and nudged Grey towards her brother who wrapped a warm arm around her as she gripped the sleeves of his shirt.

Slowly, Dimitri lead Grey back to the house with one glance back at his sister who had begun the shift back. "Are you okay?"

Grey shook her head, humming a "nuh-uh" as she walked beside the boy with shaky legs.

"You're handling this really well, you know." He laughed. "My bonded ran away when I told her. She didn't talk to me for weeks and then came back and apologized."

"Your what?"

"Nothing."

Ignoring his comment, Grey swallowed the lump in her throat as they walked inside the house and into the living room. "I need to go home."

"You need to rest." He sat her on the couch. "I'll get you some water while we wait for Petra."

Dimitri disappeared into the kitchen, leaving Grey to herself. She ran a hand through her cold hair as she sighed and dug her free hand in her pocket. Pulling out her phone, she almost cried in relief when she saw a voicemail from her work.

"Grey," It was her boss, Levi. "I haven't heard from you, in fact no one has. . . I hope everything is well. Whatever is happening that you can't seem to call your boss, I hope it is because you are too invested in your work to call me. If there is a problem that will interfere with your work, I can fly you back on the next flight. Call me back."

"You can't tell him."

Grey snapped her head to look at Dimitri who was leaning over another couch, a glass of water in one hand. He walked around it and handed the glass to Grey.

"How did you-?"

"We're wolves, supernatural creatures, doll." He smirked and leaned back on the couch. "We have slightly better senses than humans."

"Why can't I tell him?"

"The only reason we told you, is because of that picture you took of-"

"Dimitri." Petra wobbled through the front door, her hair wet and clothes clinging to her skin. "Leave before you make things worse."

"I was only answering the girls question, sister."

Petra growled and spat Russian words in a low voice that made Dimitri give her an equally as fierce growl before glancing at Grey and stomping out. Petra then flopped on the couch across from Grey and looked at her.

"Are you okay?"

She nodded.

"You are scared?"

She shook her head.

"Why won't you talk?" Petra cocked her head the side and that blonde wolf flashed through Grey's mind.

"I don't know what to say after that." Grey gave her an odd look. "Are you okay?"

Petra laughed. "I've done it a lot since I first shifted, it hurts like hell but I can handle it."

"When did you first shift?" Grey found the word left an odd feeling on her tongue and wanted to say it again and again to make it go away.

"When I was fifteen. So four years ago."

"You're nineteen?" Petra nodded. "I thought you were older. . . Then how old is your brother?"

She made an odd noise in the back of her throat. "Dimitri is seventeen as of last June. He's not my brother."

"But-"

"Do you have any other questions?" Petra pursed her lips. "Because I'm quite exhausted and I'm sure you'd like to rest."

"Here?"

"I'm not letting you walk home in this weather and after what you saw I'm surprised you'd want to walk alone, after all, we're not the only beasts around here." Grey's eyes widened and she shuddered. "I'll go get you blankets and a pillow."

When Petra returned and gave Grey her things, she was ready to walk out and sleep but the human on her couch stopped her. With a frown on her face, the girl spoke.

"Who did I photograph shifting?"

Petra was tense. "Grey, promise me you will never go in the forest again."

"But-"

"Grey."

"I won't."

Petra nodded. "Khishchnik."

"What?" Grey frowned and Petra sighed.

"The man in your picture is the predator, Grey. That's khishchnik."

• • •

"Levi? Hi, it's Grey."

"Grey! I was beginning to worry, is everything okay?"

"Yeah. Yeah, everything's going good. I've got some great photos already, I can't imagine what I'll have by the time I'm back."

"Don't work too hard, Grey, you have a tendency to overwork. Consider this a vacation while working a bit." Levi's laugh crackled through the speaker. "So is everything okay? You haven't called and I was beginning to worry."

Grey bit her lip. "No, no. Everything is fine, I've just been so entranced by the country here I forgot I had another life back there."

"You sure? Because I won't hesitate to get you on the next plane back."

"I'm sure, Levi. I'll call you if I have any problems."

"Okay, be safe, Grey."

Grey blew out a heavy breath and ran her fingers through her hair as the line went dead and she was left in silence. She'd traveled back to her own cabin early in the morning and after vigorously arguing with Petra that she was fine, the girl left her alone, but not before putting her phone number in Grey's phone. Her thoughts were running rampant in her mind as she stared out at the never ending forest in the light of day.

She looked away from the forest and down at the picture of the man's back that lay before her on the coffee table. Khishchnik. She had photographed a legend and lived to tell the tale with proof. She herself could be called a legend for living through seeing him and even that wolf who spared her the other night. Grey still didn't know why that wolf turned away; she was prey, easy prey at that, that could've been killed with a swipe of it's sharp claws and fed an entire wolf pack.

Feeling the wind pick up, Grey shivered through the thick blanket and tucked her hands back inside, eyes looking up to find, not the forest this time, but a pair of blazing blue eyes.

Part Five

The wolf was incredibly close to Grey's back porch, so close she could see each snowflake clinging to it's auburn fur. She had no doubt it was the wolf from the other night. Her heartbeat spiked at this revelation, and because it took another step closer. It wasn't growling or baring it's teeth, it's ears were perked up and it's head high, confusion shining in it's blue eyes. It made a noise at the back of its throat, almost like a purr as it's nostrils flared and it's head tilted up the slightest.

Grey was frozen as it took yet another step closer, followed by another until it's puffs of breath fanned across the wood railing of her porch that blocked her legs from it. She could now make out that it's fur had been matted with what looked like dried blood around it's mouth and on it's neck. Her stomach turned as the stench of the blood soon met her nostrils. Stumbling back, her back met the wood on the outside of the cabin as it growled, ears flattening when a shadow stumbled from the forest out of the corner of Grey's eyes.

She tore her gaze from the predator in front of her - which would've been a terrible mistake in any other situation - and her eyes met Dimitri's glossy eyes. His widened as he looked at the wolf in front of her and tried to growl but it was weak and faltered as he fell against a nearby tree, his bare body sinking into the snow.

The wolf left Grey and began to approach Dimitri's unmoving body all the while growling lowly, stalking towards him like a predator. Grey panicked and did another stupid deed; she ran towards the boy on the ground. Around the wolf she moved and stood over Dimitri's body, staring at the wolf with a hard gaze.

"Don't touch him." She tried her best to sound threatening but her voice shook.

No longer growling, the wolf glanced at the boy and back to her, huffing out a short growl before turning away and darting into the trees. Grey waited another few minutes until she couldn't see it's shadow, before she dared to turn towards Dimitri and flip him over so his face was no longer buried in snow.

What awaited Grey's eyes was not a pleasant sight. Dimitri's once flawless skin was now marred with bright red skin surrounding deep gashes down his torso resembling claws. They were thick and oozed blood all over the snow and the sight made Grey sick.

Cursing beneath her breath she grabbed his arms and began to slowly drag him, with great struggle, into her cabin. By the time the boy was in the warmth of the home, sprawled out unconscious on the floor, Grey had sweat trickling down her face as she ran around trying to find medical supplies with her phone pressed to her ear.

"Petra? You need to come over right now. It's Dimitri."

Grey hung up and quickly kneeled beside Dimitri who's eyes were swiveling beneath his closed lids. When she pressed an alcohol soaked rag to his chest, his eyes shot open and his hand snapped to her wrist, his grip tight and his eyes bright, sharp teeth bared in threat. Once his eyes focused on her, he relaxed, and laid back for her to work, but his hand never left her wrist as she worked.

"Who did this to you?" She mumbled to herself but the boy heard, his hooded eyes looking at her.

"He was mad. . ." His voice was hoarse and his breathing shallow. "I shouldn't be here. He'll kill me."

"Who?" Grey was too focused on his glazed eyes to notice the wounds on his body ever-so-slowly closing to form scars.

"Khishchnik."

• • •

Dimitri had joined the land of unconsciousness once again, leaving Grey to wait for Petra in silence. She paced the floor, her mind reeling at a mile a minute. Just when she was getting fed up, the door practically flew off it's hinges and in rushed Petra and her grandmother.

"Where is he?" The old woman was frantic and Grey pointed to Dimitri laid out on her floor. With a gasp, she moved to Dimitri's side and began to mumble words in Russian.

Grey looked at Petra who was staring at Dimitri. "What happened?" Her voice was soft. "There hasn't been an attack on our kind in ages. . ."

"He said it was khishchnik." Grey replied.

Petra paled and her grandmother's head snapped up to stare at Grey with cold eyes. "Impossible."

"He was delusional when I brought him in. He was mumbling odd things so it might not have been true."

"What he say?" The old woman stood beside Dimitri's body and watched Grey with wary eyes.

"Something about someone being mad and that, that someone would kill Dimitri because he wasn't supposed to be here. . ." Petra looked at her grandmother with wide eyes. "He didn't specify who "he" was until I asked."

"Babushka?"

The old woman viciously shook her head. "You need to leave. Go home, girl, you not belong here."

"This is my home." Grey snapped.

"America! Stupid girl! Leave Russia!"

"Babushka!"

"Ona proklyata. Khishchnik ne znayet poshchady. Ona budet mertva v techeniye nedeli." The old woman spat the words in her foreign tongue, leaving Grey out of the loop.

"Babushka, ostanovit!" Petra gasped, her fists clenching by her sides.

"What is she saying?" Grey frowned at Petra who shook her head.

"We'll be taking Dimitri and leaving." Her voice was stern and cold. "Thank you for saving him."

Then, Dimitri was - surprisingly - hauled carefully into Petra's skinny arms and taken out the door, her grandmother scurrying behind her muttering Russian words beneath her breath. And as soon as they appeared, they were gone and Grey was once again, alone and confused.

• • •

Days passed inside that little cabin without a trace or sign of life from Petra or her family. Grey didn't go outside much, seeing as though every night she looked out the window, that auburn-colored wolf was waiting outside, peering back at her from the trees. As the nights turned into day, Grey felt her sanity slipping away just watching dust collect on her camera and the day she decided to take it out, turned out to be a mistake.

She'd been bubbling with excitement to have her hands on her camera again and still being too afraid of the beast that lurks within the trees, she ended up walking into town. Whereas the town was small, it's streets always seemed to be filled with citizens loitering around, talking, shopping, working, normal everyday lives - they were oblivious to the beast. The town gave off a homely vibe, a warm feeling when Grey walked through, ignoring the stares and foreign whispers.

Yet the first morning she'd been back in town, it was quiet, there was not a single soul to be found in the streets and this made Grey uneasy. Her grip on her camera grew tight as she walked cautiously further into the square, for there the silence seemed to be deadly. She saw them, the citizens, huddled in a circle chattering quietly with shaky voices. She heard a heart-wrenching sob come from the middle of the circle and a cry out to the sky. Approaching the circle, Grey turned her camera on while the first set of eyes found her. And then the whispers stopped but the crying never did, and one by one the citizens were turning their eyes to Grey and moving away from her as she moved towards them.

She paused and frowned at them as all their eyes held this same expression of horror as they looked her up and down. When she shook it off and stepped further in, the whispers started up again and she had no doubt they were speaking of her. Yet she pushed past them and moved to the middle of the circle where all her breath left her lungs.

For there, in the middle was a woman on her knees, face red and stained with fat tears as she sobbed and screamed out in Russian. Her bony arms were wrapped around a limp body of a little boy, his bright blonde hair matched hers and he bore the same green eyes, yet while hers were rimmed red and sad, his were rimmed with dark circles that stood out on his ghostly skin and his eyes looked blankly up at the sky. He was dead. That was obvious from him eyes, even more from the long, deep gashes across his chest and stomach that oozed crimson blood, and the hole in his little neck.

Khishchnik.

No other beast would've done this, and no beast dared to linger around this area what with him on the loose.

It was then that the boy's mother looked up at Grey and her eyes met hers, the sad look leaving them and in its wake was left fire. A deep, burning hatred directed straight at Grey.

She stood up abruptly, dropping the boy's body and began yelling at Grey in her native tongue. To which Grey only backed up and shook her head, fear sparking in her veins.

"You did this!" The woman's voice became heavily accented as she cursed at Grey in choppy English. "He dead because you! This your fault!"

"I-No. . ." Grey was stumbling over her words and backing away as the woman rushed towards her.

Grey yelped as she fell back and the woman leapt on her, her hands wringing Grey's neck. She gasped for air as she struggled underneath the frail woman's body, fighting for her life. All the citizens stood by watching, not one dared to interfere. They were going to let her die.

But a growl interrupted them and everyone seemed to freeze, even Grey who was still gasping for air that wouldn't find its way into her lungs.

The woman above her loosened her grip just the slightest when her head snapped to the side, Grey welcoming sweet air into her body. She sighed and just lay there breathing as the woman scrambled off of her and in her place was a large wolf.

Grey's eyes widened, taking in the unfamiliar wolf who postured itself over her in a protective stance. The townspeople were backing away in horror, whispering in their native tongues no doubt about the girl underneath the wolf. The girl who brought the wolves.

Once they were all a good distance away, the wolf growled once more and turned to Grey, looking at her with eyes she could never mistake.

"Dimitri?" She whispered and the wolf blinked its answer. "Thank you."

With a curt nod of his large head, he backed away so Grey could stand and when she was steady on her feet, he began walking down the streets. He noticed she was still standing there in awe so he turned to look back at her, waiting. She gave a small "oh" before hurrying after him, following him all the way to her cabin where he never came inside, but just watched her walk inside and lock the door for safety.

Grey watched Dimitri through the window, give a satisfied huff and dart off into the daunting trees.

• • •

Grey found herself outside again, her camera held in her hands when it was late at night. Sleep wouldn't find her and she liked to watch the way the snow was falling lightly on the ground. It was peaceful, the world was silent and in mourning of the life it lost today. Because of her.

For awhile, she just stood on her porch, letting the wind caress her skin and run through the strands of her hair, leaving little snowflakes in its wake. She let herself soak in the smell of the outdoors once again and listened the sounds around her; the sound of silence, for not a soul dared to disturb the silent night in fear of what might come out of it.

Then it seemed that a gust of wind carried with it not only little shards of ice, but a voice. A soft voice that hummed in Grey's ear and wrapped itself around her heart that was beating wildly in her chest. "Come." The voice beckoned, it's sweet melody tugging on her hand, willing her legs to move. As it whispered in her ear, she felt her body giving in to the voice and she found her legs moving her off the porch and into the snow.

She kept moving, the voice continuing to beg her to follow until she reached the edge of the forest and with one more push, her mind was foggy and the voice whispered one last thing before vanishing.

"Your fate awaits."

{i love you guys.M xx}

Part Six

{ You There by Aquillo}{i'm in love with this song so much..}

The only sounds that filled the air, was made by her boots atop the fresh snow, and her heart pounding in her chest. With each breath, each step, she found herself further and further into the forest, unable to stop her legs from carrying her into the unknown. Every time she pushed a snow-covered branch from her path, she found her heart beating fiercer, harsher, beneath her chest.

She soon found herself in a part of the forest unlike the rest. The snow that had been tainted by delicate paw prints and the trees that housed critters that peered down at her, was no longer the same. The snow was untouched and pure, the trees towering and abandoned. The wind blew colder causing snowflakes to cling to the strands of her hair and rest delicately upon her eyelashes yet it stung her skin and made her a rosy red color.

A chill ran down her spine as the temperature seemed to drop and the silence that floated heavily in the air became eerie. And only then, when her heart was a thundering drum beneath her breast and fear coursed through her warm veins, did her legs stop and root themselves to the ground like the trees around her. She was immobile, frozen as she felt another presence join her in this part of the forest, and she could tell by the way her blood suddenly ran cold, that whoever it was wasn't anyone good.

A low growl broke the sinister peace first. She was mobile again, stumbling backwards as she watched a puff of frozen breath appear right in front of her. Her own breath was labored as a silent crunch of snow was the indication the other presence was moving, so silent that she couldn't properly focus on where it came from. Another cloud of breath appeared, this time it warmed her ear and she stumbled to the opposite side seat from it, her head whipping to find nothing. In her haste to get away, she tripped, and was sitting on her now sore bottom in the snow.

• • •

He could see the way her eyes searched for him in the dark, how frantically they moved around the area where he last made his presence known. They were beautiful; shimmering under only a sliver of moonlight. Not that they needed that moonlight, for they seemed to have captured an entire galaxy in those gray eyes and they shined on their own accord.

He blew out another breath to tease her, this time on the side of her neck. He'd been close enough to catch the little hint of lavender on her skin and close enough to hear her heart pumping and her blood rushing through her veins. It taunted him. As soon as his breath fanned across her skin, he watched her shiver before she practically crawled away, huddling close to the cold ground.

Normally, by now his prey would be quaking down to the bones in fear, they'd be crying or begging for their life into the darkness, even running. But this girl, she was unlike the others he'd preyed on. He could tell she was afraid by the way her heart pounded in her chest and the way her chest rose and fell quickly with each labored breath, yet to anyone with naked human eyes and ears, the girl would seem perfectly calm. The gleam in her eyes read mischief, as if somewhere deep inside her she enjoyed this, yet the way she stayed close to the ground showed a position of protection, as if her long legs could save her from him. She was different in that normally he felt nothing but disgust for the humans he preyed on, nothing but lust for their blood, but this girl - he lusted after more than just her blood. Her scent alone had the beast inside him raging, her presence did far more.

He had been slowly circling her, trying to pinpoint a weakness when her voice filled the air.

"I know who you are." Her voice was surprisingly steady yet she seemed to have to force her words out. "I know what you are, and I'm not afraid."

He felt the corners of his lips tilt up the slightest as he stared down at the back of her head. She sucked in a deep breath and slowly turned her head around to find him under the light of the moon a little more, his silhouette just barely visible.

She felt a stirring in her stomach when his low and thickly accented voice echoed through the trees. "You are foolish to not be afraid."

"If you wanted to kill me, I'd already be dead."

"I enjoy playing with my food."

A shiver raked her body as she slowly stood to her full height and faced the direction of his voice. "Then kill me. If I am to die, I wish to die quickly."

"What if I wish to hear you scream and beg for your life?"

"Then I would deem you a sociopath ."

"Such big words." He hummed out. "Why that long term? Why not a monster? Perhaps a beast?" His voice was deep, threatening yet she still stood her ground.

"You are a beast. You are a monster. And you are a sociopath."

"Oh I am so much more. . . Darling, I am the devil himself." His voice then appeared right behind her, whispered hotly into her ear causing her to gasp and rush forward, away from his presence.

"I beg you to end this torture. Let me go, please." Grey closed her eyes tight and stood stoic, fists clenched at her sides.

"You came to me my darling. You entered my realm, my territory and you expect me to let you walk free without a scratch?" His voice was venomous all of the sudden. "I am not a merciful man."

"So I've seen." Her eyes opened and focused on his figure in the dark of the night. "Why'd you do it?"

"To whom? The little boy or that mutt?"

"Anyone?! What have they done to deserve a death or beating so vicious?"

"One's family had wronged me. The other got too close to what I deemed mine long ago."

Grey's breath hitched. "What did Dimitri's family do?"

His chuckled echoed into the air, one not of amusement but almost taunting. It made Grey shiver. "I may not like his family but that mutt is the one getting attached to my things."

"And what exactly is yours?" She was no longer scared, he could see it in her eyes. He didn't like defiance but somewhere deep down it aroused him.

For some reason, she was waiting for him to claim her as his, but he was silent. Yet the way he looked at her with those eyes of his, she knew his answer. She knew it was her. She didn't want to believe it, that the beast wanted her, so she waited for him to say it, to make it realistic. As of now, belonging to him was just a theory. A simple thought.

"Get out of my territory." He suddenly snapped at her and she flinched.

"I thought you weren't merciful?" A smirk broke out on her face. "What happened to the beast?"

His growl was one of anger, he was growing tired of her games and wanted her throat in his jaws. "I will not hesitate to kill you."

"Then do it."

"Why not put up a fight? Everyone else does."

"I'm not stupid. I know there is no use when you're far stronger than me."

"Smart girl." He smirked once again, his anger still lightly there.

Grey didn't speak another word, she didn't beg her life, she simply stood as still as she could with her eyes squeezed shut. Then it seemed to all disappear; the cold breeze, the threat that lingered in the air, him, she almost thought she was alone and he'd left. But she wasn't foolish. She felt her hair being brushed away from her neck and her lips parted, a shaky intake of breath following the feel of his fingertips grazing her skin. His sharp inhale was shortly followed, his exhale fanning across the length of her neck causing her to shiver.

Grey braced herself for what pain would come, but the only feeling that arrived was the blazing trail of heat left behind from this man's lips on her neck.

"What the-!?" Grey roughly shoved herself away from the beast and spun to face him. She was ready to yell at him, scold him but as she turned, his entire presence vanished from the forest as the first rays of daylight made the snow at her feet shimmer like diamonds.

What had just happened?

•

"Grey?" A voice broke through the air from around the front of the cabin. It was Petra, she'd knocked but there had been no answer so she walked in. She could smell Grey in there so she didn't know why she didn't answer. "Grey? Hello?"

Petra walked carefully through the cabin and into the back where she pushed open the bedroom door with a long creak. Her room was dark, the curtains had been pulled shut and the lights were off, but with the light flooding in from the rest of the house now that the door was open, Petra could see her in the dim lighting.

She was sat on the edge of her bed, hands rested limply in her lap and her feet planted on the ground. Her eyes were wide open and staring off into space towards the wall. She didn't budge.

Petra's voice was filled with worry as she addressed Grey with reserved caution. "Grey. . ."

Grey didn't move, she didn't even blink. The only indication of her being alive was the steady beating of her heart and her soft breathing. So Petra continued onwards until she stood in front of a frozen Grey, when she crouched in front of her, she placed a hand over one of hers. She gasped at her frozen skin.

"Grey!" Petra shook her gently. "Grey, you're freezing cold! Snap out of it!"

Petra quickly moved and grabbed the duvet off her bed and wrapped it over Grey's shoulders before sucking in a deep breath to brace herself for what she was about to do.

"Sorry. . ." She almost whined out before her hand made contact with Grey's cheek with a 'crack!'

Grey gasped and blinked a few times, a pale hand coming up to cup her cheek in shock. Her eyes soon found Petra who stared at her with a guilty expression.

"What the fu-"

"You were zoned out, Grey. You wouldn't move or blink or anything! I had to." Grey stayed silent. "What happened?"

She didn't answer.

"Grey, what happened?"

"I saw him."

"Who?"

Grey snapped. "The predator-beast dude! Kisha-whatever you natives call him! I saw him last night in his human form!"

"Human?"

"He wasn't that wolf that he always is. He was purely man and he was taunting me, speaking to me in the forest. He. . ." Grey's voice trailed off as her hand came up to brush her fingers across her neck.

Petra's eyes stared at her neck for the longest time, almost as if she was searching for something, before she sucked in a breath. "How are you. . .-"

"I don't fucking know Petra! But something tells me you or your creepy grandmother knows what's going on and I want to know."

"Grey, I-"

"Don't you dare lie to me, Petra." Grey's eyes were welling up with tears. "I feel like I'm going insane."

She sighed and ran a hand through her hair. "Come on, let's get you by a fire first. You're frozen."

Part Seven

Everything around her seemed to be frozen in time. The world became one big blur of bland colors swirling around her as her head spun. The real world, reality, became nothing but a big blur of fake, that she had lived happily surrounded by her entire life. The real world was gone. And the only words that she heard were spinning around her head, they were the words that Petra spoke only seconds ago. The words didn't seem to leave her mind, they imbedded themselves in her brain and taunted her with their dangerous meaning.

The girl had called it 'just a theory,' a mere idea, a thought that she had conjured up one night and hadn't been able to forget since. But something about that so-called "theory," had dread chilling Grey's blood and freezing her body.

"It's just a thought - a theory at that - so don't overreact okay?" She had started. 'Not overreact, my ass.' Grey thought, but nevertheless let her continue. "I believe that you two may have bonded - possibly unintentionally."

"Bonded?" Had been Grey's immediate response with a tilt of her head.

"It's when the soul of your wolf sort of morphs or forms a connection with another soul. If my soul was to bond with some villager's soul, I'd feel an immediate pull towards them - an attraction - and it won't go away until me and that villager have mated. Even after that it'll still be there." Petra sighed. "In most cases, it happens between two lycans, a human bonded to a lycan is rare; even rarer for a human to be bonded to lycan as powerful as him." She didn't need to say his name, Grey knew who he was.

"So you're saying the soul of his wolf," The words felt odd leaving Grey's lips. "chose me to form some weird connection with and now I'm his?" Petra nodded. "So I am his without any say?"

"No, Grey whenever the first time you two met was, he was intrigued by you and he couldn't figure out why you drew him in. And the times after that was him figuring it out and you accepting it."

"I did not!"

"You accepted it the second you walked in that forest after I told you countless of times not to." Petra's voice was stern and it made Grey snap her mouth shut.

She twiddled with her fingers a little bit before speaking. "Mating is-?"

"Sex, basically."

Grey paled. "So you expect me to have sex with that beast out there?"

"No, okay, it's a theory. It's the only logical reason that he'd let you live and almost murder Dimitri unless he wants to watch you go mad; which could also be a possibility but let's go with the first option."

"No let's not."

"Having someone to love you for eternity isn't all that bad, Grey. . ."

"Someone to love me?! Someone to love me!" Grey's blood began to boil. "You've said it yourself; he's a monster. How am I expected to love a murderer? He wants me dead, I know it! He just enjoys fucking with my head! It's impossible for him to want to love me and it's impossible for me to love him!"

"Grey, please calm down okay? Let me explain."

The girl snorted and crossed her arms, her eyes giving a quick roll before glaring at Petra. "Please do."

"In those books you've read, they might've mentioned something about rodstvennyye dushi or soulmates. Those books are outdated and a bit fictional, but there are some truths. They get the soulmate part pretty spot on besides the fact that the authors believed that these 'mates' were predestined but they're not; you don't necessarily get a say but the soul of your wolf chooses who to bond with and there's an instant attraction."

"So he picked me? Out of anyone in the world. . . Me?" Petra nodded slowly. "Why?"

"I don't know. Something about you drew him to you and now it's inevitable. He won't be satisfied until he has you." Petra shrugged and when she saw Grey paling again, she added: "Just remember, it's not for sure."

Grey groaned. "How can we know? I need to be able to leave in a few months. I have a life back in New York!"

"I don't know. . . We'd have to have you two meet again, and I'll have to be there to see how he reacts."

"I'll go into the forest again-"

"Too dangerous. . ." Petra then trailed off her eyebrows knotting together and her eyes glossing over. "That just might work."

"We'll put you in a dangerous situation. If you two are really rodstvennyye dushi then he won't stand idly by as you are attacked."

Grey looked at Petra like she was mad. "What if he's six towns over and I die?"

"I'll be there, just close enough to jump in if I need and far enough to stay undetected." Petra shrugged. She had it all planned out. "And anyways, if you are bonded he is never too far from you."

"How is this gonna work?"

• • •

"You'll go into the forest. . ."

Petra's voice echoed in Grey's mind like a broken record. Her words from earlier never stopped replaying; leaving Grey to ponder what future the world holds for her. Had she just been brought into this world to be a submissive lover to a beast of a man, who might she add, was supposed to only exist in children's books. She didn't want to fall in love with a beast, but even she couldn't deny the strange attraction she felt towards him; but she had just thought it was because she had always been into troublesome boys. He was the definition of trouble.

Although she'd been in the forest many a times since she'd arrived in this country, she shouldn't have felt nearly at home in this eerie place. Yet even with Petra's presence lingering not far behind, she felt chills travel through her body the further she got away from the parts of the forest she had grown fond and familiar of. Now the trees were thicker, closer together making it harder to see far ahead. Their leaves made a thick block to keep out sunlight and the still air was far colder.

"Stop here." Petra's voice bounced off the trees and Grey obeyed, planting her feet firmly on the ground.

"When we arrive at the destination, we'll run into a wild gray wolf who should be hostile."

The moment Petra's presence disappeared to God knows where, another body filled the void--the gray wolf Petra had spoken of. It was small and skinny and it's fur was matted. When it growled and snapped it's jaw at Grey, thick strands of saliva flung off it's teeth and dripped onto the snow below. It was rabid and wild, no remorse or mercy held in its dark eyes.

Had Grey not known that far more terrifying beasts lurked in the shadows of this very forest, she would've been terrified. But now she was calm. Too calm in fact, and that scared her more than the wolf that could end her life growling at her.

"Whatever the wolf does, don't move. Look into its eyes until it steps forward then start to run. It'll chase."

The little wolf circled her a few times, continuing it's obnoxious snarling before it took a step forward and Grey flinched, yet here eyes never left its eyes. This angered it and its fur puffed up and ears flattened out against its head, it was giving her one last warning to not challenge it. It took yet another step. And another and another, before Grey finally willed her legs to move and ran further into the forest, away from where she came.

"When you run, be loud, stomp your feet, run so fast that you're gasping for breath. Make your presence known to him and make it known that you are in danger."

Grey's left hand held her camera still from bouncing around and the other pumped back and forth as she sprinted through the trees. She hadn't even made it that far and she was already panting, legs already aching. I need to work on my cardio, goddamn.

She took a sharp turn to her left and ran a few more meters before she felt a sharp pain shoot up her leg from her calf. She cried out as she tumbled to the ground and found herself pressed between the snow and a snarling wolf hovering above her face.

Her breaths were now labored and hid a slight whine as her leg grew numb from the pain and the cold snow. As the wolf growled in her face, she cringed and tried to shove it off but it didn't budge despite it's small stature. Her arms felt heavy with fear and no matter how hard she banged on it's chest and pushed, it wouldn't budge. She brought her hands up to push at its face; a big mistake. It's jaws clamped down on the hand that tried to push it away and she screamed.

"If anything goes wrong, I won't be far. Just yell."

"Petra!" Grey yelled into the empty forest for her friend, tears streaming down her face like the blood that ran down her arm and leg.

When she yelled for her friend again, the wolf was at it's wits end and dug it's claws deep into her stomach causing Grey to scream at the top of her lungs and try to kick the wolf off. But Grey was weak, she could feel the blood staining her skin and clothes and she was no match for even the smallest wolf.

Where had Petra gone? Was she as wounded and close to death as Grey? Had the beast got her?

Grey's mind was littered with thoughts as she felt the fight leave her body as her limbs went numb; whether it was from pain or the cold snow, she didn't know, all she knew was that her body was floating on nothingness.

But she was relieved that she couldn't feel anymore, because she knew that death would slowly creep up on her with no savior near, and she would welcome its cold tendrils. No Petra, and no bonded beast to save her from a terrible fate. The wolf still stood above her, growling at her frozen form, watching her carefully. It was searching for any sign of life but Grey guessed there wasn't much with how it didn't make any moves to finish her off.

Each intake of breath was a pure whine and her exhales were shaky and quick. She winced when the wolf pressed down on her wounded stomach and sucked in a shocked gasp. The wolf grew angry again. She watched through hooded eyes as the wolf brought his lip up in a snarl and as his head dipped down towards her neck her eyes squeezed shut, preparing for death.

Part Eight

I t all stopped the moment she closed her eyes.

The pain was gone, the weight of the wolf on her chest, the fear. Everything disappeared and was replaced by a crippling silence. She felt nothing, not even the cold snow surrounding her body; not even the wounds that littered her body and left her surrounded by crimson snow. Why this was, she didn't know, but Grey welcomed the peace and took in a deep breath.

She lay there as she released the breath in a sigh, her body completely relaxed. She took this as death but when a sound so eerie erupted her silence, she thought she might be in hell. The sound repeated again, a cross between a deep moan and a loud sob echoed in her ears over and over until she realized that sound was coming from her. She was crying, sobbing so hard the only thing she could feel was her body shaking.

Then it seemed reality came flying back. She was thrown back into a world of searing pain and a heaviness in her lungs. Her own sobs weren't the only sounds reaching her ears, they simply muffled the sound of skin being torn from the bone, yelping and growling. There was a battle happening meters away from her but she was paralyzed by fear and pain she was unable to move and watch the scene unfold. Even if she had wanted to see what awaited her, she couldn't, her body was still shutting down and death's cold hands were wrapping around her.

By the time Grey's breathing became slow and shallow and her body had grown numb from the cold, the sounds had all stopped and left was a heavy panting. Snow crunched beside her under a large weight until there were puffs of warm air fanning across her clothes. Above her body then loomed a large wolf, a familiar one at that, one that sent shivers down her frozen body and caused a stirring in her stomach. It was khishchnik.

He simply stood there, panting heavily with blood matting the fur near his mouth, his bright eyes watched Grey who was frozen in her place. As much as she wanted to move away from the beast, she was unable; the pain having paralyzed her as well as the realization that Petra's theory was true. He didn't want her dead - he'd saved her from that fate - he wanted her. Plain and simple.

Somehow she found her voice, it was barely there, raspy and thickly laced with pain, but she still managed a snarky remark to the beast who could end her life in the blink of an eye. Little did she care, because mythical creature or not, what could he do to save a girl already in death's grip?

"Is this your way of playing with your food?"

If beasts could smirk, she would've sworn those lips had curled into just that. And that scared her; more than werewolves being real and more than one wanting her, the fact that a wolf could smirk shook her to her core. For it was a sinister sight to see before her eyes rolled to the back of her head and her body succumbed to the eerie whispers of death.

• • •

Grey was drifting between the land of the living and the land of the dead. Her eyes fluttering open occasionally to look at the branches of trees intertwining above her, watching curiously as they passed her by. She thought for a moment she was floating until she registered the slight shake in her body and the arms wound beneath her back and knees. She tried to move, to fight whoever was carrying her, but her arms were limp, draped across her still-bleeding stomach and the other swinging through the air by her side, dripping little red droplets of blood in their path. Her lungs still felt heavy, her breathing shallow and wheezy. She was barely holding on to life, a tiny sliver of light in the darkness called death that had surrounded her.

Her head lulled to the side on a particularly heavy step, away from the treetops to see the old barn in Petra's backyard through eyes that she struggled to even crack open. Standing on the back porch of their house was an frail old woman who she knew as the grandmother of Petra, and beside her stood Dimitri who looked paler than the snow at their feet. His eyes were on her, taking in her graying skin and bloodied body with a little fire of anger in his eyes.

Grey's eyes fluttered shut as they neared, open long enough to see the old woman glaring at whomever carried her. As the feeling slowly creeped back into her body, she began to shiver violently, the cold finally reaching beneath her skin, yet the pain was still gone and for that she was thankful. The arms supporting her wrapped around her tighter and she found herself practically curled against a heated chest. She breathed out a content sigh at the smell of the forest radiated off the firm chest and invaded her senses.

"I thought we had a deal." The chest rumbled with each word and if Grey had control over her body, she was sure she would've hummed against it.

"I apologize for my granddaughters reckless behavior. It won't happen a-" Petra's grandmother spoke smoothly, a hint of irritation on her tongue but she was cunning enough to hide it.

"No you don't understand, Klara." The unknown voice turn hostile. "She almost got killed. If I hadn't stepped in she'd be dead. Your naïve grandchildren have already broken our deal twice. If it happens again, she is mine."

Grey could imagine the fury blazing in the old woman's eyes as she spoke. "No. You don't understand. She does not belong here or to you. She is from America, she has a life. You cannot just take her because that beast inside you wants her blood."

The chest her face was pressed against rumbled as a vicious growl left his lips. "We want more than just her blood. She will be mine, Klara. Your grandchildren are stupid and she is too curious for her own good. She follows the pull too easily and it will lead her back to me always. You cannot stop it." His voice was almost sensual, yet there was a threat underlining his words.

After a moment of silence, Klara spoke. "Dimitri, take her inside."

The chest she was against rumbled violently, yet again in an animalistic growl. "I don't want that mutt's filthy hands on her."

"He won't hurt her. She's freezing, she needs to be inside if you want me to heal her." Silence. "She will die if you hold onto her any longer."

There was a silence and she felt her body leave the warmth of the stranger and into the arms of who she guessed was Dimitri. His warmth nothing compared to the stranger.

The stranger spoke again. "What's her name?"

"Her name is Grey."

Their voices began to fade as Dimitri took her away, yet nothing could've stopped her from hearing the way the stranger's Russian tongue spoke her name.

"Grey." He paused again. "I'm trusting you, Klara."

"You have my word; she is in good hands."

And as the voices became silent, nothing but the sounds of her own shallow breaths and Dimitri's footsteps, she realized who the stranger was. She realized why his voice was so oddly familiar and why the feeling of him felt so right.

It was him.

It was khishchnik.

• • •

When Grey finally came to, she found herself on an unfamiliar bed with Petra sitting beside her reading a book. She stirred and Petra's head snapped up.

"Welcome back to the land of the living." She set down her book and smirked at the girl.

"I died?"

"No, thanks to yours truly." Grey frowned at her. "If I hadn't saved your ass, that wolf would've had you six feet under."

Grey simply stared at Petra, not because she was shocked, but because something deep down was screaming "Lie! She's lying!" And for some reason she believed it with all her being.

Why did she lie?

"What about khishchnik?"

"He never came Grey. . ." She hesitated and the smirk on her face faltered a bit. "I guess you two aren't bonded."

"But-"

"I'm sorry, really Grey. I shouldn't have jumped to that conclusion and put you in a dangerous situation like that." Grey noticed the way her eyes glazed over. "I've just been waiting for the day I become bonded and I overreacted with you."

Grey frowned. "You're lying."

"No I'm not." Petra became hostile. "Go shower and I'll bring you food when you're done."

With that, Petra climbed off the bed and walked out the door, leaving Grey alone and confused on the bed.

After a few moments to gather her thoughts and bottle them away, she finally tried to sit up and shift, but the pain in her abdomen left her breathless. With a tight knot between her brows and a shaky breath, she pushed herself up carefully and stood to her full height.

The door to the bathroom was open and the light illuminated the little room. Shutting the door behind her she began to carefully take off her ripped and stained clothes. What once was a gray T-shirt, now bore four stripes down the middle and a large patch of red. Grey shuddered.

After stripping bare and starting the shower, she noticed the rusty colored bandages wrapped around her stomach, hand and leg. She first removed the wrap on her hand, the holes where the wolves teeth had imbedded themselves were still slowly oozing with blood yet they looked days old, not fresh. She breathed, and with shaky hands, she unraveled the other bandages until her skin shone under the bathroom light. She felt nauseous as she looked at herself in the mirror. The skin on her stomach was red and irritated, surrounding four jagged scars that were roughly the length of her own hand.

Grey then realized that the wound on her leg as well was not even scarred, but gone. She remembered the wolf taking a good bite from her skin yet there was no trace of it ever happening. She'd been attacked yesterday, and her wounds that almost killed her looked like they happened months ago. Running her fingers over the scars on her stomach, she frowned as she felt a jolt of electricity pass through her hand; sparks almost.

After a long and thoughtful shower, Grey emerged with a newfound sense of determination and stormed downstairs with her hair dripping onto her clean clothes. Finding Petra wasn't hard, she was sat next Dimitri, whispering to one another in their foreign tongue. Upon her entrance, they looked up, eyes wide.

"How am I alive?"

"I saved-" Petra began.

"Don't you dare lie to me, Petra." Grey's voice was fierce. "I'm tired of living in the dark. Just tell me what's really going on." Grey watched Dimitri hurry from the room.

The girl hesitated before giving Grey a small smile. "Grey, are you okay? That wolf must've done more damage than we thought."

"Petra what are you-"

"Grey, there was no one else in those woods but you and I. Khishchnik never showed up. I saved you."

Grey felt her heart skip a beat. "No you didn't! I was screaming your name but you didn't show up! I saw him, Petra."

"No you didn't. Grey, listen to me-"

"He was there. He carried me here. He was talking to your grandmother." Grey continued to talk, Petra simply shook her head.

"Grey. You were dreaming. He was never there."

Grey felt like she was losing her mind. "Yes he was! I saw him, Petra!"

"I'm going to get my grandmother, stay calm." Petra quickly stood and walked out as Grey broke down.

"I felt him, Petra. I felt the bond."

Petra stood frozen in the doorway for only a moment before she continued to walk out and away from Grey. Her presence was soon gone from the entire house and Petra's grandmother, Klara, was wobbling into the room to put Grey in a magic-induced slumber.

{sorry i've been slow with the updates.. i've been reading a whole bunch on here and i've been writing not one but TWO new stories which i am SUPER FUCKING EXCITED ABOUT and i can't wait to debut them after they are finished as well as this. i love you dudes.stay safe. }

Part Nine

After being trapped in Petra's home for two days with only a wild six year old and a silent four year old, she embraced the feel of her camera beneath her frozen fingers. She didn't known how it had made it out of the woods without a scratch, but she was thankful it was in her hands again. Outside, the cold air tickled her throat with each intake of breath, but she embraced the crippling silence and the smell of the outdoors. The frozen land of Russia was beginning to grow on her and she couldn't imagine how hard it would be when the time came to go back home. But she did miss New York, and its electricity and the warm covers of her own bed, the only thing she didn't miss was all the noise. Out here, in the middle of nowhere, she felt like she could breathe without the crowds of people and she could think properly without the constant honking of horns and loud voices.

Pulling her camera up to her face, the sound of the shutter snapping frames filled her ears as she stared at the rundown barn in Petra's backyard. She'd missed this - taking pictures, it was something she'd been in love with since she was young; the way a moment could be frozen forever in time. All her happiness and sadness had been documented on this camera of hers.

Moving her view to the ominous forest, a shiver ran down her spine as she took more stills of the frozen world. The trees stared back at her, not moving in the wind as if they were watching her too. She'd never seen such eerie trees before, yet they intrigued her and she found herself taking as many pictures of them as she could. After taking a few more shots of the spacious backyard, she stood in the middle of the yard and flicked through the pictures she'd just taken, assessing them with careful eyes.

The pictures were dark to say the least, that ominous vibe radiated from even the pictures. But pictures didn't do the world here justice. With the cloudy sky and an a abandoned barn in front of a dark forest, the pictures looked like scenes from a horror film. As she scrolled through the pictures, she felt a strange feeling settle in the pit of her belly, as if her body was warning her for what was to come. But she brushed it off as nothing and continued scrolling through her pictures with pride.

It was then she noticed something odd about the pictures of the tree line. In the seemingly black and white world, there was a spot of crimson red that pooled at the base of the trees. Looking up at the real world with wide eyes, she could see the outline clearly - a body laying at the edge of the tree line. How she hadn't noticed it before was beyond her, but the dread in her stomach warned her not to investigate.

But Grey was Grey, and she was curious and there was also something that overpowered that fear and pushed her to get closer. So, she slowly approached it, her legs heavy. The closer she got, the more she could make out. A small body; a child with brown hair. A boy, with his back to her and his face to the trees, blood covering and surrounding his body. When she was feet away, all breath left her body as she looked at him. It was as if her pounding heart was an alarm inside of her, screaming at her to run away but she couldn't hear it.

Carefully she rolled him so he lay on his back, the wounds on his small chest visible. But it wasn't the deep gashes down his chest that sent dread down her spine, it was the fact that they were identical to the ones on her stomach, yet they were larger, deeper. This was not the scrawny wolf that had almost killed her but one with power, one far more dangerous. And she had a feeling deep in her gut that she knew exactly who it was.

But not even that could scare her more than his eyes. Lifeless green eyes that stared up at the heavens. Green eyes that once held life and a spark that she had seen with her own eyes. For there, in the crimson snow, lay Ethen.

"Petra!" She sobbed, backing away from the boy. "Dimitri! Someone help!"

Petra was running towards Grey the moment she heard her cry, her grandmother and Dimitri with Rosalie on his hip were behind her.

They found the girl at the edge of the forest, on her knees sobbing in front of a body. Petra's pace faltered for a moment, " what would have her like this?" her mind was rushing with possibilities as she continued and regretted it almost immediately.

"Oh my god." She choked as Grey turned to her with a pale face and red eyes.

Petra pushed past Grey to the boy and fell to the ground, taking him in her arms. "No. No. No." Her hand hovered over the claw marks that tore deep into his small body, shaking with the fear that froze her body. She was holding her little brother, his lifeless eyes now looking at her.

"Ethen!" Rosalie cried out. The little girl had pushed out of Dimitri's arms and ran to Petra's side. "Petra what's wrong with him?"

But the girl didn't answer, only stared at her little brother with wide eyes. The little girl stared at Ethen for another moment before turning to Grey with pleading eyes, as if she was asking her to save him. When Grey didn't do anything, Rosalie rushed over to her grandmother and wrapped her little arms around the woman's frail legs.

"Who did this?" Petra whispered, her voice broken.

"Khishchnik." Klara's voice was grim. "No other wild wolf near us is big enough to leave marks this deep. . ."

Petra then looked up at Grey as her grandmother took a crying Rosalie into her arms. Grey stayed crying quietly a couple feet away from the boy and her.

With venom on her tongue, she spat. "This is your fault."

"Petra-" Grey looked pained.

"You did this! You killed him!" Petra screamed and stood up, eyes blazing. "This is all your fault! He's dead because of you!" Grey was shaking her head, crying.

"Petra, stop it!" Klara said.

"If you hadn't come here, he wouldn't be dead! This is your fault." Petra then lost it, trying to lunge for Grey who screamed and tried to scurry away.

Dimitri's arms encircled Petra's torso as she tried to attack Grey. She growled and clawed at his arms, her attempt to free herself. It was then that Petra broke down into hysterics, body going limp in Dimitri's arms as she sobbed.

"Petra, I'm sorry." Grey said softly, shaking her head.

Through sobs, Petra managed. "Just go."

"Petra-"

"Leave!"

"Dimitri, get her inside." Klara said, her hand rubbing Rosalie's back.

To Grey, the world was spinning and her ears were ringing, the only thing visible were Ethen's eyes now looking at her. She could her the little girl sobbing into her grandmother's neck and her own heartbeat. She heard Klara calling her name from a distance.

"Grey." She turned to Klara who gave her a sad look. "I think it's time you went home."

Grey nodded and began to stand.

"I mean home. I think it's best if you go back to America."

Grey felt her heart break as she nodded - too out of it to hear the growl that shook the trees. "I'm sorry."

"Don't blame yourself. Khishchnik is more beast than man. Nothing can tame him."

• • •

When Grey got back to her cabin, she packed her things and sat in a quiet home and just cried. Never before had the girl felt so alone. She simply sat there, on that old couch in silence late into the night when her sobs had subsided and turned into hiccups. Even then, the feeling of loneliness had settled deep in her veins and she was left numb and staring blankly at the far wall. She felt like life had nothing in store for her anymore. She felt like there was no point anymore.

And those feelings and silence could be a dangerous combination. A combination she hadn't felt in years. Years before she made it to New York. Years before she barely even made it. She was scared deep down, because the last time these feelings had taken over her, her thoughts turned dark and had she not been such a coward she would've listened to them and not made it out. In the silence of her cabin, Grey sat not only in the darkness of the night, but the darkness of her mind.

And then, the silence was broken by a long howl from nearby. The sound alone sending chills down her spine, coaxing her out of her episode. It was a howl that called out to her. It whispered with the wind long after it stopped and it left Grey mesmerized with it's voice. Another howl, this one long and low, closer than the last that left strong emotions floating in the silent night. It left her breathless. It kept calling out to her, so Grey stood and slowly made her way out on the back porch, where the wind bit her skin and seemed to whisper in her ears louder, more forcefully. Had she been in her right mind, she would've turned around and went inside, but the tear trails on her cheeks and the blank look in her eyes showed she was out of it; and the tugging in her chest told her to go into the dark trees, just like that little voice that the wind seemed to carry. So without any source of light but the big full moon looming above her, she went into the forest with the thought of seeing the man she knew as khishchnik again.

While her thoughts should have shook her to the core after what happened earlier, they didn't. The thought of encountering the beast again sent her heart thumping wildly beneath her chest. She didn't know why: why she felt this way or why she was even going into the forest again, but she didn't try and stop any of it. So she deemed herself mad, all sanity gone and in it's place a hollow shell of insanity. No soul should crave the presence of a beast, let alone his touch. To feel her skin on his skin again, the thought alone gave her the sweetest kind of chills that made her toes curl. Grey accepted it, she had lost every bit of humanity and common sense in her body, and she was okay with it because that meant she got to see the beast one last time before she returned home.

{this is short but I tried to lengthen it but it was actually really hard. if it was to be longer it would've had to be completely rewritten and i like the feel of this chapter a lot.}

Part Ten

From the moment she stepped into those trees once again, she was deemed his. No longer protected by the witch, she was his to ravish and do as he pleased. The deal he had made with the witch was broken, and he was allowed to do whatever the hell he wanted.

Klara was a powerful witch, she had felt the girl's soul and had seen early on what she was destined for the moment she stepped foot on Russian soil. She was quick to wind her magic around the girl, protecting her from the beast who craved the human so viciously, of course this had infuriated him but he was powerless against her magic. She didn't know why he'd chosen her, but he did and that wasn't something even the most powerful magic could change. She was destined to be his and he'd be killed before he let her get away, even then the beast would fight for her in the deepest pits of hell. He had fought for her the minute he had figured out she was to be his and he couldn't have her; that's where the deal came in. Despite the great lust he felt for the girl, he didn't like the idea of having this girl around and he didn't want her near, so he let the witch protect her, but his beast wasn't happy. So he gave her three strikes, if the girl is in his territory or in danger three times, she is his. The witch was supposed to protect her and that entailed protecting the human girl from even him.

Deep in the forest, Grey had no idea he was there, yet she unintentionally following him until she was officially in his territory, and only then did he make his presence known underneath the dim light of the moon.

"We meet again, moya l'vitsa." His words were smooth and he could see the fear glimmer in those eyes of hers for a second before it disappeared and was replaced with simply nothing - nevertheless that fear for him was there deep down and he lived for that. "You should know by now that the forest is dangerous at this time of night."

"I'm not afraid of you."

He growled out his words. "Ne lgi mne. I could sense your fear the moment you stepped into the trees. You cannot fool me."

There is a silence that settles over them and he uses this time to look her over. Even clad in thick sweatpants and a large coat, he can still feel the flame of desire lick up his spine. Her wild hair and bright eyes have him imagining what she'd look like after a night with him. His thoughts run wild with images of her bare legs wrapped around him as she cries out his name in bliss, her hair even more a mess from his hands pulling it and her eyes dark with lust only for him. The beast inside him raged at these thoughts. It wanted her desperately.

She was still silent so he spoke, beginning to move around in the darkness. "You know, you are a fool to come into these trees alone. A beast could take you as his and you'd never see the light of day again." There was something else in his words, Grey could hear it.

"You'd let them take me away?" She was playing with him, the predator now becoming prey. "You'd let a beast ruin me?"

He growled. "I cannot stop a beast once it has been unleashed."

His words made Grey shiver but she never let her fear show through. She titled her chin up and raised a brow at the trees. "Then show me, beast, what I have to fear. Come into the light."

He knew deep down that she wanted him to deny her request and disappear into the trees, her braveness only a façade, a protective shell to keep the innocent girl from being ruined. Deep down she feared him, she'd probably rather die than be with him, but even deeper down he knew she wanted him just as bad as he her. So he stepped forward, until his entire body was drenched beneath the light of the moon, watching her as her eyes widened just the slightest and burned a path over his entire being.

•

Her eyes took every inch of him in. Despite his large body being hidden beneath a thick flannel and jeans, she could imagine that every part of him was rippling with muscles. He was tall, broad shoulders and a strong jawline, his lips were pink and full, a sharp nose rested between those two blue eyes she came to know so well. His hair was dark, unkept and wild - just like him. He was mesmerizing.

Grey was silent, staring into the eyes of the man otherwise known as a beast, khishchnik, a murderer. All these thoughts were running through her head, but nothing could stop the rapid beating of her heart as he stepped closer, not from fear but from excitement. He stepped closer and closer, his bare feet sinking into the snow; he was trying to scare her. He wanted her to run away in fear, so he could chase her. He wanted her to be the prey to fit so perfectly to him. He wanted her blood to taste even sweeter after fighting for her.

She lifted her head higher, trying to seem brave but her façade faltered when he was toe to toe with her, his breath fanning across her forehead. He reached a hand out, tucking her golden hair behind her ear.

"You are afraid, I can hear your heartbeat."

"How could I not be even the slightest, standing before a murderer?"

He growled, low in his chest, his eyes narrowed on the human girl. "Watch your tongue. You'd be smart to turn around and go back to Klara now before you regret it."

"What are you going to do?" Grey stood her ground, red hot anger slowly filling her veins. "Kill me like you killed those little boys?"

"I'd do far worse to you, darling." The way he spoke the word 'darling', the way his lips curled into a grin made Grey shiver. Yet the image of those sinful lips covered in the blood of the innocent had her shivering with fear.

He shocked her when he grabbed her by the shoulders and spun her around. Eliciting a gasp from Grey, he tightened his grip on her shoulders and pressed her body firm against his as he leaned forward.

With each word he spoke, his breath fanned across Grey's ear and slithered down her slender neck. "We've had this conversation before, do you not remember?" Grey's body was tense against his, afraid of moving the wrong way and angering him, or worse. "While the thought of ripping your pretty little heart out pleases me, I'd rather do much more. What I wouldn't give to get inside that head of yours, to possess your entire being, to hear you beg for mercy, to beg a beast to kill you. When I said I like to play with my food, I meant I like to see it suffer before I end its life."

Grey ripped away from him, spinning around when she was a good few feet away, only to find he was gone. She knew he was still there though, for his presence was one of a thunder cloud; causing so much turmoil without physically touching anything. She didn't realize she was crying until a sob left her lips and she sank to her knees.

"Why does a brave girl cry?" His voice was behind her, but she didn't turn away. "I thought she didn't fear anything."

"You've ruined me." Her voice was broken, a weak whisper. "I don't even know your name, but you've ripped apart my life more than anyone I've ever met. You haunt my dreams in the most amazing ways, yet I still fear the beast that you are. I am afraid of you, I admit it."

He approached her slowly, until he was looming above her kneeled form. He then leaned down just enough to lift her chin so she peered up at him. His gentle touch took her by surprise, even more by his soft tone. "I am not a merciful man, and neither is my beast."

Grey frowned up at him, utterly confused. "What?"

"Go back to your cabin. Do not enter the trees again." He dropped the hand under he chin and became rigid.

She stood and shook her head. "I can't."

"You will, or I will have your heart between my teeth." He snarled as if to add effect.

Despite her tears, she emphasized each word with the tiniest bit of venom. "I can't go back."

"What do you mean you can't?"

"Petra blamed me for you killing her brother. . . I'm going back to America."

Rage filled the man before her. "Why did she blame you?"

Grey hesitated. "She just said if I had never come here, you never would've killed Ethen. The woman in the square practically said the same thing when you killed her boy."

"Why would they say that?" His eyes narrowed on the girl.

"Petra thinks we've 'bonded' or whatever it's called. She said that's the only valid reason that you haven't killed me."

He was tense. "Like I said before, I enjoy toying with my food."

"Well I guess you're gonna have to hunt down some new food." Grey gave a small smile, attempting to ease the mood but if anything, the air grew colder.

"I do not waste my food. I will not finish until I am fully satisfied." He walked closer to Grey, who backed up further and further. "And we are far from finished my darling."

With that, he closed the distance his large arm wrapping around Grey's waist and pulling her flush against him. Her eyes widened as his head dipped down to her neck and he inhaled. Grey was ready to push him away but when his lips then brushed across her skin, she froze, a delightful shiver making her toes curl.

"What are-"

Grey's voice was cut off when a burning pain ripped through her shoulder and down her spine. She cried out, pushing away at the man who's face was still hidden in the crook of her neck. His body was stoic and her attempts to push him away failed, his jaw still locked on the crook of her shoulder. She flailed until her body grew weak and she lost all fight, slumping against the beast's solid body. When he finally pulled his face away, his mouth was stained red, sharp canines peeked from behind those lips, dripping with the same red; her blood.

His eyes were on fire, as he looked down upon her with hooded eyes, filled with sensuality. Those eyes seemed to have captured the light of the moon within them, they burned so bright she felt like she'd go blind staring at them for too long. But they were enchanting and they left her breathless.

"'Ty moya."

{bitch finally grew some balls and claimed her. *sigh*

Where are you guys from?? I'd love to see how big our little world is and where my writing has reached. ;))

all my love,M xx}

Part Eleven

{ i'm so incredibly overwhelmed with all the comments on the last chapter, hearing where all of you are from is amazing. some of you are actually probably really really close to me and some of you come from places i have literally never heard of and idk that's just amazing. so thank you all, from the bottom of my heart. i appreciate every single one of you. also enjoy this update from your very hungover author who's birthday is today ;))}

Petra's heart was broken, barely beating. She could hardly be considered a person with the way the bags under her eyes had darkened and her cheeks sunken in. She walked around like a zombie, all life drained from her eyes and had been replaced by the cold eyes of Ethen's. That image haunted her dreams and every waking moment of her day. It was as if the image had not only burned itself into her brain, but taken hold of her and every time she looked in the mirror it was as if Ethen's dead eyes were staring back at her. That had been her little brother, one of her last few living connections with her parents - with her dad - and now he was gone. Yet somewhere deep inside she was able to find peace because she knew that Ethen had been reunited with the parents he probably didn't remember in someplace grand. He was at peace.

It had taken a lot out of Petra to muster up the courage to come to Grey. After her anger had disappeared, in its place was grief and regret, a deep sort of grief that chilled her bones. She felt bad for blaming the murder of Ethen on Grey, because in reality he'd probably wandered off too close to the trees and the beast that lurked within was hungry. And in all honesty, it was Petra's own fault, she was supposed to be watching him. She didn't want to lose Grey, she had grown fond of the human and didn't want to see her go so soon, so here she walked down the road to Grey's temporary home.

Walking up to the cabin Grey stayed in was like walking down memory lane. The cabin that was now long abandoned and dark, was once bright with the flames of the fireplace and loud with the laughter of a child. Petra remembered what it was like the first time she walked up these steps; she had been but a little girl and was chasing after a bright blue ball that had blown onto the property with the wind.

She remembered the door opening to reveal the little boy with a tuft of blonde hair and big brown doe eyes peeking out from behind his mother's thin legs. She remembered his mother's voice, warm and smooth like honey as she asked her for her name.

"Well Petra," She had said as she tugged the boy out from behind her and in front of Petra. Even two years behind the girl, he was taller and skinnier than her, her ball held in his boney fingers. "This is Dimitri. I hope you two can become friends."

When Petra returned home that night, bounding with glee but her grandmother was furious. She told her to stay away from that family, that death hung over their heads like a cloud and she was not losing Petra too. She had told her, "Do not talk to the little wolf ever again." Her grandmother had claimed darkness followed the little boy too, but Petra found it hard to believe that such a scrawny little thing could have a terrible fate. Then, days later, the little boy was found crying in the middle of the towne square, sat in front of his parents mauled bodies. He became a member of their family after that, despite her grandmother's grumbles of displeasure.

Petra shook the memories away and moved up the steps, after knocking on the old wooden door, she recrossed her arms snug against her torso and waited patiently in the cold. Minutes passed and there was no sign of movement so she knocked again and got the same reply as before.

"Grey?" She called through the door, her hand moving to the cold doorknob.

Turning the knob, she found it unlocked and pushed open the door with a creak. She knew it was wrong to barge into ones home, but there was an uneasy feeling that had settled itself in the pit of her belly. Upon walking inside, she found the cabin cold with abandonment and the feel of the air on her skin made her shiver. Grey had already left. She didn't even get the chance to apologize to the only friend she'd ever made outside her own home.

With a sigh, Petra discovered Grey's scent still lingered in the air, she must've left last night, she thought. Moving around the cabin, the scent trail led Petra to the back porch where she peered out at the forest's trees. It seemed that Grey's scent continued into those trees, but when Petra began to turn to go back inside, she caught the barely-there outline of a footprint, almost completely erased by the fallen snow.

All breath left her lungs before she ran back inside and into Grey's room to find all her bags packed and sat on her bed. Her bags were here but she hadn't been for a good few hours. Why?

Then it dawned on Petra like a slap to the face.

She never left to go home. She's still here.

●　●　●

Grey found herself staring up at the tree branches once again, at the way they intertwine and wrap around one another. The sun was shining through the treetops, so bright the snow was ever so slowly melting. Knitting her eyebrows together, Grey tried to move her arm but found her body weak, all her energy drained and it took everything in her to just twitch her fingers. Her whole body ached and screamed with the tiny movement. It was then that every memory came back to her and she shot up in shock.

Not only did her head begin to spin, but a sharp pain shot down from her neck to her toes. When her hand came up to clasp her neck, she found the skin there was raised and sensitive to touch, but covered with dried blood that stained her shirt and skin down her shoulder and chest. It was then, she also realized she'd been in a patch of her own bloodstained snow. Her hand moved to cover her mouth as she looked around at what could've easily been considered a murder scene.

She should've died. What he did should have killed her.

As reality hit her and the slight pain in her body settled in, Grey began to cry and she didn't stop until her body was shaking and the setting sun was turning the sky pink. Grey had never been a crier but lately it seemed it was all she ever did. When her cheeks were stained with tears and her eyes grew so puffy they were hardly open, she turned her head up to the canopy above and peered through the branches at the sky. And staring at those first stars of the night, Grey begged to whatever higher power there was looking down on her for a better life than this. And then, out of nowhere came that sinister little voice that blew in with the wind, beckoning her forth.

"Come." It whispered in her ears, wrapping it's soft tendrils around her neck, caressing her skin and seeping into her skin making her relax. It's sinisterly sweet voice tugged her onto her wary feet and begged her to follow it into the dark trees.

The voice continued to guide her, to whisper in her ear, to possess her mind and body. And Grey continued to beg it to stop, to leave her alone, but the voice only got louder and more violent as it tugged her over fallen trees and under low branches. She tried to struggle against it, to plant her feet or even slap herself out of it but she couldn't move her limbs, it had taken over her being and was left to watch it destroy her.

"Stop it!" Grey cried out. "Please, stop."

The farther into the forest she walked, the farther away from the hope of ever returning home grew. She told herself she was going to die out in the trees. As the snow became thicker and the white mountains grew bigger, Grey felt her body begin to hum. It lit up like a flame and left Grey breathless. She let her eyes close as she sucked in a breath and shook her head, terrified of what was happening.

"Come." The voice sung from the trees, echoing in her head.

The voice began to laugh a laugh so sinister it stopped Grey in her tracks, the spell broken. It was a laugh that shook her to her core and she knew it would forever be imprinted in her brain, its sound and the feeling it left her with. The laugh grew louder as she began to panic, looking around for any sign of life. Grey fell to her knees and covered her ears, eyes shut tight she begged the voice to go away once more. And with one final command from the now screaming voice, everything was gone and Grey was left alone in a part of the forest she didn't know.

Her eyes shot open at the sound of a twig cracking to her right. She uncovered her ears but stayed frozen, staring at the ground in fear of what might be there. A laugh then came from the same point as the twig, yet this time it was something that would haunt her dreams and leave her shaking in fear, it was the laugh of a child. An innocent child.

Jerking her head up, all breath left Grey's lungs at the sight of what stood in between two thick trees.

"Ethen?"

Part Twelve

"E then?"

The little boy giggled and covered his mouth with his tiny hand, his green eyes seemed brighter, glowing almost. He removed his hand to let it fall to his side and stared at Grey with a small smile playing on his lips. He tilted his head to the side at her before he turned and darted off into the trees.

"Ethen!" Grey was up on her feet in seconds and running after the small boy.

Around and between trees he weaved, Grey hot on his tracks. Deeper and deeper the little boy ran and despite his small legs, it seemed as though she could never catch up to him, he was always just out of her reach. The sound of his laughter filled the forest and slowly drove Grey insane. She was calling his name, pleading with him to stop but he kept running. Deep down, she knew he was dead but if he was then how could she see him so clearly?

"Wait! Ethen, come back!"

The boy took a sharp turn and vanished completely behind a tree. There was no giggles, no little footsteps, nothing to indicate that he was ever even there. And everything grew silent despite the sound of Grey's ragged breaths, and she felt the heavy weight of loneliness settle in once again and she felt like breaking down. She was officially losing her mind, from hearing voices in the wind to seeing the dead, there was no way she was sane.

"Grey." A voice whispered in her ear and she spun around to find nothing but tall trees. "Grey." Again behind her but there was nothing.

"Stop it!" She screamed. "Leave me alone!"

"Grey?" Ethen was standing behind her, and slowly turning around she saw him standing there with his hands over his chest and eyes wide and sad. "What did you do to me?"

"What?" Grey stuttered over her words.

His little hands moved away from his body, covered in blood from the wounds on his chest that poured blood down his body. "Look at what you did to me." His little voice whined out the words and his lip was trembling in a pout, tears welling up in his big green eyes.

"No." She was shaking her head and stepping back.

"How could you, Grey? I thought we were friends?"

"It wasn't me! It was the beast!"

It was then his voice grew loud and deep, almost demonic. "You are the beast! You, Grey! You!" Grey was sobbing as the boys face morphed into something otherworldly, he was no longer an innocent but something straight out of nightmares. His eyes were pale white, no pupil, no color to the iris, just white and his face was scrunched up into a vicious glare.

"No! Leave me alone!"

Hands wrapped around Grey's torso and she fought as Ethen vanished into thin air. She kicked and screamed and clawed at the thick arms wound around her waist.

"Stop fighting me, woman." The chest against her back rumbled with every word, his voice all too familiar.

Her entire body froze as the arms loosened up enough to spin around and stare up at blue eyes.

"It's not real." He spoke so soft she had a hard time believing this was the same man who called himself the beast.

Despite all that he'd done, she took comfort in his warm embrace and fisted the thick shirt he wore and buried her face in it, eyes wet with tears.

"I wanna go home." She said.

After a moments pause. "You can't."

Grey pulled away as the mark on her neck began to burn. She put a good few feet between their bodies and her hand snapped up to her neck, his eyes following that hand.

"What's happening?" She grew dizzy, eyesight blurring. As he stepped towards her, she put a hand out to stop him. "No, stay away from me."

He didn't stop his approach though, his eyes that blazing blue color, as if blue flames were dancing within as they assessed her, his canines seemed to be sharper, larger, behind his plump lips and this scared Grey. He approached her like the predator he was.

Grey tried to stagger away but her body quickly grew weak and soon the world was nothing but a black haze.

• • •

It seemed that the moment he touched her, the forest became alive. As if every tree, every creature, every being underneath the shade of the tall trees had their eyes on them, watching them in awe.

"A girl?" They all seemed whispered to each other, soft voices carried with the wind. "A girl."

Every living thing in that forest knew of his affliction, and to see him carrying this girl deeper into the trees and not out of them was like a dream. For just like him, they were all cursed too, even the trees. The little creatures may not have been able leave the cursed forest like him, but they didn't carry the curse in their blood, it just surrounded them. For him, it burned in his veins each time the moon grew big and full in the night sky, every waking moment of everyday, and each time he touched her.

She could save them all, break the curse placed upon the land and free them all. But she had the hardest of it than any other being in the forest, for she had to learn to love a beast, a beast incapable of any emotion. A beast who had taken the lives of so many innocents. A beast who can't even love himself, expected to love a girl as much as she loved him, before time ran out.

• • •

He didn't know why he was carrying her deeper into the trees, towards his home, but he was. Maybe it was because of the way she talked back to him, maybe it was because she didn't fear him, maybe it was because he liked the way the fire burned within her eyes when she spoke to him, as if she liked the danger of being near him.

He glanced down at her, her long eyelashes hid those magical eyes of hers. Never before had he seen such a color, a shimmering silver that on some days he'd noticed was a light blue. He had taken his time the first night she came into the forest to truly see her, to scope out every detail of her face that he could see, and he had been mesmerized. She had brought upon him feelings; emotions that he didn't want to ever feel again.

The wind grew harsh and the world grew colder the further he walked, for the journey to his home was a long one. The cold wind began to turn her skin pink and she turned to hide her face in his chest causing him to tense. He could feel her warm breath through his shirt and he felt like his control was slowly slipping away from just the feel of her breath. He couldn't imagine what would happen if she looked at him a certain way. He silently vowed to himself to not lose control in the way the beast wanted, if any control was lost it would end with her life being taken, not her innocence.

The sight of the old castle shadowed by the trees was a relief to him, it meant he could distance himself from the girl and still know she was safe. He looked upon his home, the ivy that grew up the gray-colored stones and the west wing that had been destroyed long ago and now was simply a ruined structure hanging onto the rest of the home. Pushing through the large front door, he kicked it shut and made his way up the winding staircase and down one of the many hallways to an empty room, one of the smallest ones around but he didn't know how long the beast inside him would keep her alive for.

Setting her down on the bed's white duvet, he stared down at her as she nuzzled her head into the large pillows, his focus on the way her slender fingers gripped the pillow as if it was keeping her from floating away. And standing there he wondered what she was dreaming about, whether it was good or bad, and all of the sudden his thoughts took a turn to the darker side and the beast inside raged for control. He pushed him down and stormed out of the room, slamming the door behind him.

• • •

Grey shot up with a gasp, the chirping of birds filling her ears from the open window to her left. With wide eyes she looked around the unfamiliar room and froze, trying to hear anything but the sound of her own breathing, but there was nothing. She was alone, so she thought, and decided it best not to sit around and admire the small yet elegant room, but to find a way out.

As she stood, she noticed her feet were bare and her boots and socks had disappeared to god no where, but shoes were her last worry. In fact, if anything, Grey was grateful to be barefooted as it helped her to move about with stealth she normally didn't possess.

Grey came to find the only unopened door - the open one led to a spacious looking bathroom - for in the room was unlocked and it opened without a sound. Creeping into the long hall, she didn't bother to close the door behind her and instead moved as quickly and quietly as she could down the burgundy colored hallway, pushing down the urge to take in all the paintings on the walls. At the end of the hall, she found another hallway across from her and a grand staircase in between the hallways. Deciding the staircase was her best escape route, she slowly descended the stone stairs and at the bottom, she hurried to the double doors that were twice her height.

Her hands were on the handles for just a second before they were ripped away and found her back now against those very doors and a large hand wrapped around her neck. Her own hands gripped the stranger's and her nails dug in his skin but he didn't loosen his grip.

"Kak vy syuda popali?" He snarled down at her as she gasped for air, his dark eyes glaring at her.

Grey tried to push out words but his hand around her throat prevented any from forming. She tapped his hand repeatedly, as if trying to tell him she couldn't speak let alone breath but he didn't let up. Squeezing her eyes shut, Grey tried to suck in as much air as she could but none would come through and she felt her head begin to spin.

On the brink of unconsciousness, the man's grip let up, just enough for her to suck in all the air that her lungs could handle. He repeated the Russian words again but Grey shook her head.

"English." She managed out and he frowned, putting a little more pressure on her neck.

"How the fuck," The man's accent was thick with anger filling each word like venom. "Did a girl like you find this place?"

"I don't know."

He growled low in his throat and it was then Grey realized he wasn't human. "Lie to me again and I'll have your blood painting these walls, human."

"I swear." Grey stammered out as she gasped in more air, her hands back to clawing his. "I just woke up upstairs."

The man was now furious, eyes a pitch black color seemed to shine and his jaw was clenched so tight, Grey thought it might break under the pressure. His grip around her neck became impossibly tight to the point where Grey wasn't even gasping or fighting, she just stood there like a fish with her mouth wide open and her eyes teary.

She closed her eyes, preparing for the end when she heard a loud growl that shook her to her core and all of the sudden she was on the ground in a coughing fit. In between coughs she'd gasp, trying to make herself feel normal again. Still in her fit, she looked up to find the man who had just been choking her was now in her position across the room. The man with his hand around his neck had his back to her but Grey had no doubt who it was by the way her body began to buzz. Khishchnik.

They were having a glaring match and with a vicious few words in Russian, the beast dropped the stranger who looked at Grey with a venomous glare before he stormed off leaving a now silent Grey alone with the beast. He turned slowly to face her, those blue eyes burning as bright as always.

"Where am I?" Her voice was rough and her neck was throbbing but she didn't care as she pushed herself to stand on wobbly legs. Her slender fingers gripping the doorknob as support as well as a quick escape.

He was silent for awhile, simply staring at her hand that was carefully holding her neck. "Home."

"My home is thousands of miles away." Grey said slowly.

"Not anymore." He turned and began to walk away when her voice stopped him again.

"Who was that?" She asked. "The man who-" Her hand hovered over her aching neck.

"That was my brother."

Part Thirteen

"**M**y brother."

With a lingering stare and a curt nod, the beast strode up the stairs, leaving Grey alone in the foyer still holding her aching neck.

She sat for a few moments, bewildered by everything that has happened in a short amount of time. It seemed within the short span of time she'd been in this foreign land, her life in New York had been but a dream and no longer existed. This impossible life was hers now and it felt as though there was no escape from the horrors and unexpected events in it.

Almost forgetting her previous mission, she shook her thoughts away and stood slowly, shocked that both men left her completely unattended. As if one hadn't almost killed her in the middle of escaping and the other didn't care. Fools, they were.

Turning slowly, her eyes still on the stairs and the doorway where the brothers disappeared to, she placed her hands on the door's handles and pushed one open slowly. No sound came from the door or the gigantic house so Grey took her time to stay quiet and sneak out the large door.

Once outside, she carefully closed the door and spun around fully prepared to run but she was frozen.

The sound of birds chirping above the light snow filled her ears. Most of the snow was gone, but there was enough on the ground still that no green grass peeked through. Winter was over and spring had come with a bright afternoon sun and heaps of wildlife hiding in the shadows of the tall forest trees. Taking in a deep breath, Grey relished in the scent of the fresh air that had lost it's bitter bite.

A deep, menacing growl from inside the castle broke Grey's trance and a shiver of fear ran down her spine. She wasted no time, breaking off towards the trees in a dead sprint, ignoring the forest's rough ground hurting her bare feet. She had no idea where she was or where she was going, but nowhere was better than being captive. Grey could hear multiple sets of footsteps and she supposed both men were catching up to her and fast. She had to do something.

Taking a sharp turn to her right and deciding then to zigzag her way through the forest, she gained some space but not for long. She could hear rushing water, and hoping for an easy escape, she headed towards it.

The trees grew taller and the forest grew denser as she ran, making everything harder. Her calves were burning and her lungs felt like they were about to collapse and now she had tree branches that were digging into her skin to push aside. Yet the ever present growling behind her pushed her to go faster.

Determined to get home, Grey didn't realize that the world had completely turned around on her and the sound of water was gone far behind her. The forest was playing tricks on her, it wasn't letting her leave. With the beast hot on her tracks, she began to feel dread settle in her veins, all hope of getting home was dwindling to but a dream.

A scream ripped out of Grey's throat as the ground suddenly gave away and she was tumbling down a hill, sharp rocks and fallen tree branches dug into her skin and ripped her bloodstained clothes. During the tumbling, a sharp pain had followed the sound of a snap and she was left screaming as she rolled. After reaching the bottom of the hill, Grey lie still, trying to regain her shaky breath, tears streaming down her face at the pain that blossomed from her foot. Her chest burned with each intake of breath but she could see a black wolf atop the hill, watching her with eyes the color of a burning flame. She knew it was the beast's brother by the way those eyes held so much anger and disgust, he looked ready to leave her there for dead. But of course, fate wouldn't have it that way and he was emerging from the tree's shadows to stand behind the wolf, those entrancing blue eyes watching her and in that moment, she knew he wouldn't let her go.

So despite her burning lungs and the new trails of blood that stained her skin, she pushed herself up on aching muscles and tried to keep as much weight of the foot that had already swelled up twice its normal size. She was trying her hardest to move, walk, even hop away but everything was against her and she found herself on the ground once again. This time she was spun around so her back took the brunt of the fall, instead of her face thank god, and now hovering above her was the notorious beast. She grunted out her frustration and gave him the best glare she could muster up.

"Why won't you let me go home?" She asked with a shaky voice as he scanned her injured body, slight annoyance slipped out on her tongue.

"It's not me, it's the trees." He spoke with a mischievous gleam in his eyes.

"What?"

"They want you just as bad as my beast does." He leaned his head down to where there was a mark on her neck. She grew stiff as his nose ran over the spot and he inhaled her scent. "Maybe when I'm done with you, they can have you."

A shudder ran down Grey's spine as a gust of chilly wind shook the trees above them. She was about to speak when the black wolf behind them growled, bright eyes fixated on something far behind the two on the ground.

The beast above her growled as well, watching his brother move forward as a stealthy wolf, hidden in the shadows.

He spoke rough and low. "My dolzhny vernut'sya brat."

Grey watched the wolf that was now beside them huff and snarl towards the trees once more before taking off. The beast then moved off her and grabbed her limp hands, tugging her to one single unsteady foot, the other lifted off the ground.

His eyes took their time traveling to her injured foot, scanning carefully over every contour of her body making her squirm. When his eyes snapped back up hers they were glowing. "It's just a sprain. You can walk."

He began to tug her forward but Grey pulled away, hands free from his electric grip, grabbing onto the closest tree to steady her unbalanced self. His head cocked to the side and one eyebrow quirked up, his face no longer hidden by the human mask; she could see the wolf hidden underneath the sheep's skin.

"We must go back, woman."

Grey shook her head and gripped the tree harder. "I don't want to go back."

"You came into these very trees for a reason. There's no turning back, these trees are more unforgiving than I."

"I don't understand."

He was in front of Grey in under a second, eliciting a gasp from her lips. "The trees have eyes. They have their own souls. I may be a beast, a monster, whatever you wish to call me, but this forest would swallow you whole, darling. Those souls of theirs are just as dark, if not darker than mine. They like to watch you humans go mad." Grey's eyes showed her fear and he smirked. "Now, now, where's the fire I saw in your eyes when you spoke to me by the town? Where'd that little lioness go?"

He held out a hand to Grey who swallowed her fear and glanced at it with wary eyes. "What is that?"

"If you wish to get lost then don't take it."

"I can't walk even if I wished to hold it." She gestured to her foot.

"Like I said, it's just a sprain." He rolled his eyes before his body tensed again and his eyes snapped to the trees not far from them.

"Why are the trees moving?" Grey's voice was soft and quiet, afraid to disturb the nightmare that had become reality.

"I told you, these trees are cunning, they will do everything in their power to separate us, because they can toy with your mind, not mine. Now come here before I leave you for the trees to drive you to insanity." His voice was venomous as he looked upon her with dark eyes.

"I can't-"

A shriek left Grey's lips as he scooped her up in his arms, her own unintentionally grabbing onto his neck and hair. He winced and growled, the hand supporting her back moved quickly to slap her hands that grabbed his hair before splaying against her back again. Her grip on him loosened, hand leaving the silky strands of his dark hair as he began to walk, all the while grumbling in Russian beneath his breath, no doubt cursing her.

...

Back at the castle, the beast had dumped her on the couch in a little room connected to the foyer and left her alone once again with oh-so-sweet parting words.

"Try to run again and I'll let the forest do what it does best."

He was gone again, stormed off in a cloud of anger that seemed to always hang over him. He was a mystery, a corrupt soul that Grey secretly wanted to save but didn't know where to even begin. He was so far gone, she didn't know if there was a chance of bringing him back, let alone enough humanity left in him to even hope for the good to overpower the evil.

With a sigh, she swung her legs to rest against the floor and stared at the foot she had sprained, it was still swollen and had scratches from the twigs and rocks she'd ran over in her attempted escape. The entire length of her legs were covered in little scratches and even her arms were as well, her clothes ripped in some places to reveal scratched and irritated red skin beneath, little spots that would form colorful bruises littered here and there. She stood slowly, applying pressure slowly onto the foot and when it didn't give out underneath her weight or cause her great agony, she walked cautiously to the stairs. At the top where the stairs broke into two, she found herself staring off to her left, to the hallway she hadn't come from originally. Something inside of her was pushing her to go there, to explore each room until she'd memorized every detail of that hall. But that little voice inside one's head appeared and told her no, not to disobey the beast, not to push him off the ledge, for when he is destroyed, she'd surely be taken down in the end along with him.

So with a shake of her head she carefully moved back down the hall, where the room she left earlier was with it's door still open. Yet this time, the difference was that by the door were the very suitcases she'd left by her bed, packed and ready to return to America back at the cabin. And atop them all, her camera case and the glasses she's been so desperately needing alongside a note with messy handwriting.

Grey,

Forgive me and my brother for our behavior. Join us for dinner at 7.

If you do not show at the exact time, I will not hesitate to drag you down here and force food down your throat myself.

Don't tempt me, lioness.A

{translation:

•My dolzhny vernut'sya brat.translates to "we have to go back brother"}

Part Fourteen

{ here he is. the wonderful, the rude-at-first-but-is-totally-sweet, older brother of the beast. (His name is revealed in this chapter) portrayed by Jon Kortajarena. *major heart eyes*}(this throws back before Grey woke up and was almost choked to death by the brother)

He had traveled back to the little cabin that the girl had resided in after leaving her sleeping on a bed. The journey wasn't too long, but with clever trees changing the winding paths and the up and downhill parts, it proved tiring. All he wanted to do was return back to the girl, despite his attempts to push these strange feelings down, they always resurfaced. He despised it and her for making him feel these things.

Coming upon the cabin, he had not expected it to be buzzing with life. He could see them all in there yelling, their faces etched with worry. He recognized Klara's calm face amidst the chaos, shaking her head at something the skinny blonde girl was yelling. The boy who he'd attacked before, Dimitri, was leaned against the couch inside staring at his shoes as a little blonde girl ran around, her tiny voice humming reached his ears along with the others argument.

"I know he has her, babushka!" Petra yelled. "You know it too yet you sit here and let us do nothing!"

Klara stared at the girl. "If khishchnik does have her, then we cannot get her back. This same thing happened years ago and the girl never returned, Petra. Let her go."

"No!" Petra yelled, tears brimming her eyes. "This is my fault! I can't sleep at night because all I see when I close my eyes is her in Ethen's position. Laying lifeless in her own blood and her eyes-"

She choked on her own words and began to sob, Dimitri moved to her side, wrapping his arms around her so she wouldn't collapse.

All eyes were on Petra as she had her meltdown but his eyes were on the little girl who had made her way out of the cracked back door and stood on the back porch staring at him. Her little eyes gave away no fear, but curiosity as she took a step off the back porch. He growled at her in warning but she only smiled a wide smile with many missing teeth. Then, she giggled and ran inside, gaining the attention of Klara who's eyes immediately found his.

She excused herself and made her way to the trees in front of him. "Why have you returned?"

"I came to retrieve her things."

She pursed her lips. "Are there no clothes left from-"

The growl that rumbled in his chest was a warning. "Give me her things and I will be gone."

Klara nodded, hurrying inside and returning back outside with empty hands, he growled at the sight. "I put her things outside her window. If Petra saw me touching her things, she'd throw another fit."

He huffed. "Keep her under control, Klara."

"She will come searching for Grey." Klara said with sad eyes. "No amount of magic can stop her from loving that girl you've got in your castle. When she comes for her, don't you dare harm her."

"My actions depend on hers. If she barges into my territory trying to take what's mine, I will not hesitate to kill her. Your blood or not, if she tries to take her it will be her blood on the ground."

"I know."

• • •

"What the fuck were thinking?" His brother glared at him from where he stood in front of the stove. "Bringing a girl here, let alone a human girl!"

"She knew we existed thanks to her own curiosity." He said with a bored tone. "She has a camera and she captured a picture of me shifting."

His brother's eyes grew wide. "You shifted out in the open?"

"No, I was in the forest." He sighed. "She carries no fear in her body for the darkness in these trees. It was inevitable."

His brother growled. "Is she coming down or not? I will not delay dinner because your pet is stubborn."

"Watch your tongue, brother. If she's not coming down, it's most likely due to your sweet greeting this afternoon."

"How am I supposed to react to a stranger in my home? This house holds history, it holds secrets that I promised to protect at all costs." His brother made himself a plate and sat down at the table. "Even if that means killing this girl."

The beast leaned forward and watched his brother like the predator he was. "You do know she can break the curse?"

"Do you think me ignorant? I was made aware of that when I saw she had breasts." The beast growled low. "I am just not ready for these games yet, not after what happened last time."

"We are running out of time dammit!" He slammed his fist on the table and his brother looked up from his meal. "Maksim. I have lived almost three decades with this curse, I refuse to die with it."

Maksim stared at his brother who'd always had a worse temper than him. "Can you manage to love her though? That's the real ques-"

His dark eyes darted up to the doorway where the girl stood, her body tense as she entered the hostile air. Maksim watched his brother lean back in his chair and rake his eyes up and down her long, lean body.

His brother spoke. "I was beginning to think you'd never come down." He wore that dark smirk as usual.

"I was hungry." Her answer was curt as she moved to where the food was and piled it high on her plate. She began to walk back out when his voice stopped her.

"Where do you think you're going?" Maksim could hear him growing angry but the girl just stared at him with a glare in her eyes.

"To my room."

"I asked you to dine with my brother and I as an apology." He spoke through gritted teeth.

Her gray eyes darted to Maksim, who was in the middle of stuffing a large part of his steak in his mouth. He looked back at her with those judgmental dark eyes and cocked up a brow.

"I'd prefer to eat in my room." She said, her eyes going back to the beast who was now standing and moving towards her like she was prey.

"That wasn't an option." He growled out. "Now sit."

There was a fire in her eyes as she now stared up at him, their faces inches apart. "I am not some dog who is going to obey your every command. Do not tell me what to do."

Maksim watched his brother's lips curl into a smirk and his eyes take on that familiar glow. He stood and prepared himself to step in at any moment.

"I believe you hit your head too hard on that tumble down the hill, darling." He said as his fingers trailed across her temple and her fingers tightened on the plate in her trembling hands. She was skilled at hiding her fear, Maksim would give her that. "No one tells me what to do."

"You're a fool if you think I'll sit idly by after you kidnapped me and treat you as if you are some long lost royalty!" Her eyes were full of fire. "You are nothing to me."

She rolled her eyes and Maksim watched almost in slow motion as his brother snapped and the plate in Grey's hands dropped to the floor where they once stood. But now she was pressed against a wall, with his brother's body covering hers, his teeth sunken into the mark on her neck.

Maksim let his brother's name slip past his lips, but he was too focused on the feeling of Grey's body against his and she was too focused on the pain that coursed through her veins like fire to catch the name clearly. He called out to his brother again as he ran closer and got no answer.

Maksim ripped his brother away from Grey making her yell out in pain as his teeth tore a trail into her unmarked skin. He caught the girl before she tumbled to the floor and she grabbed onto his arms like they were the only thing keeping her alive. He glanced down at her, making sure the shaking girl was okay before looking back up to find his brother gone, no trace of him left.

He growled low in his chest and looked back down at the girl.

"Can you walk?" He asked and she looked up at him with glossy eyes.

"Please don't hurt me." Gone was the feisty girl from earlier and left in her place was a girl with a voice no doubt as broken as her.

He rolled his eyes. "I'm not going to hurt you if you don't act stupid. Come on, I need you to try to make it up to your room so you can lie down."

With a hesitant nod and a shaky breath, she straightened out and began to walk slowly beside Maksim. He took the time it took to reach the top of the stairs and the end of the long hallway to take in the girl, trying to find what it was that drew the beast of his brother to her. He could see the appeal in many of her features but seeing her like this - broken and covered in her own blood - there was nothing but pity for the girl. Pity that of both of them, she got claimed by the brother with the most darkness in his heart.

Leaving her sat on the side of her bed, he hurried into the bathroom and came out with a wet towel. She was still sitting where he left her, shaking and pressing her crimson hand against her neck. Without any words, Maksim moved her hand away and pressed the towel to the wound, as she sat there twiddling her thumbs trying to forget the pain.

"What's your name?" She spoke softly, her voice raspy.

"Maksim."

"I'm Grey."

Maksim pulled the towel away to inspect the wound and couldn't help the feeling of guilt that flooded him when he caught sight of the faint bruises on her neck. That was his doing.

She saw where his eyes were looking. "Don't worry. . . It seems as if life has thrown every near-death experience at me. Yours was nothing compared to what your brother has put me through in this short amount of time." Grey then spoke with a laugh yet there was no humor in her words. "So is the biting and the blood something I should expect from your kind?"

"Remarking is a common thing, it's meant to show affection and in cases like this, assert dominance." Maksim walked back to the bathroom and returned with a tiny first aid kit. He dug through it until he had some bandage and what looked to be tape. "The first time you're marked, of course there's blood, but after that there should only be a little. His teeth were still in your skin when I pulled him off you, it caused it to tear into your skin that wasn't marked."

"Is it going to scar?"

"It'll probably end up looking just like your mark." Maksim spoke while he closed the first aid kit and set it on her nightstand. "Get some rest, it'll help.

"Thank you."

His dark eyes met hers and he saw the sincerity in hers. "Don't thank me yet. I helped you now but this was hardly a glimpse of what my brother can do. Don't let him break you."

{and the nameless beast is still a mystery... any guesses to his name??}

Part Fifteen

The next few days passed in a blur. Most of Grey's time was spent in the room she slept in, staring up at the ceiling, memorizing even the tiniest of details on the walls, furniture and even floors. The only time she left was to make the long and lonely walk to the kitchen to always find every meal cooked and placed on a porcelain plate ready for her. She'd sit on the cushioned ledge in the bay window and stare out at the slowly melting snow as she ate, watching spring fast approaching. Her friends would begin to worry. She thought often about escaping, trying to run again but the fear of those magic trees was far greater than the beasts that lived under this roof. So she decided to wait.

A week passed like this, with Grey slowly going insane with no human contact. She thought she'd made a small break towards friendship with the gloomy Maksim and would've even enjoyed a 'hello' but there was no sight of him or even the beast. She secretly waited for him to come storming down the stairs and into the kitchen every time she ate; she wanted him to just look at her with those blue eyes that haunted her dreams. Even a glare she'd be thankful for.

She just wanted to see someone beside herself everyday.

On the eighth day, after she'd cleaned off her plate from breakfast she made her way up the stairs, stopping at the point where they broke into two. Staring at the stairwell to her left and that always dark hallway that called to her. She could feel her heart pounding in her chest as she debated on going back to her cave or exploring the many rooms this little castle held. It seemed then that her feet had been possessed and with her heart pounding beneath her chest, she climbed the stairs she'd never touched before.

At the top, the hallway she found was - in most ways - similar to the one she'd been up and down a thousand times. The same burgundy walls and dark tiled floors yet this hall only held but five doors and not a single piece of artwork adorned the walls. There were four doors spread along evenly - two on either side - and the last one, a beautiful set of double doors was placed at the very end of the hall.

There was something about those double doors that had Grey ignoring all the other doors and making her way down the hall. Upon reaching it, she noticed how it went all the way to the high ceiling and from corner to corner of each door were beautifully carved designs, a story swirling beneath the haunting images. Wolves were carved in the wood, wolves running, wolves howling, wolves tearing each other apart. Few Russian words were written here or there but her eyes couldn't leave the image of a wolf with it's teeth in the neck of a human woman.

With a heavy breath and that image burned in the back of her mind her hands fell on the brass handle of one door. Whipping her head around, she looked back to the mouth of the hallway, expecting those blue eyes to be watching her with that ever present anger. She was almost waiting for him to walk around that corner and grow angry at her and yell at her to stay away from this place; something about this hall felt so forbidden.

Her fingers pushed down the handle and it clicked open, echoing down the hall. Pressing a palm to the intricately carved wood, she pushed the door wide open with a long creaking noise.

Creeping inside, her flats made the only noise against the tiled floors before she shut the loud door as quietly as she could and was engulfed in darkness. Pressing her hands against the wall, she moved them all directions until she found the light switch beside the large doors and flicked it on. A dim glow from a stunning chandelier lit up the light blue walls and gray tiles beneath her feet.

All breath left Grey's lungs as she took in the room, adorned with a large white rug in the middle and two white loveseats sat back-to-back atop it. There were a few statues carved from granite in the corners but what really caught her eyes were the portraits that lined the walls.

She moved slowly around the room, admiring each person, more stunning than the last, their clothes becoming more and more modern than the last with their names carved in delicate script beneath the pictures. Each man and woman carried the same surname: Volkov.

She stopped in front of one of the last ones, a woman who left her entranced by her sheer beauty. Pale skin and chocolate eyes and hair darker than the night. Her rose colored lips held a smirk as if she knew every secret of the world. Grey's eyes left the eyes in the picture to her name, but there was none, only a blank slate where it should have been. Her head tilted to the side as she stared at the woman as if she'd seen her before. There something about the woman that she was sure she'd seen before.

With a shake of her head, she turned to the final two pictures; another single person and a family. Beside the mystery woman was the portrait of a man with blue eyes so cold it made her shiver. His graying dark hair was slicked back and his mouth was set into a scowl atop a sharp jaw, with a crease between his brows. Under the man it said, "Gregor Volkov".

With one last glance at the man's chilling eyes, she looked at the family portrait. In it, was the same mystery woman standing beside Gregor who wore that same scowl, while the woman held this time more of a soft smile as the hand of hers adorned in fabulous jewels was placed lightly in Gregor's, while the other rested upon the shoulder of a stone-faced little boy. The two boys at their feet were quite opposite; the taller one wore a smile and an expression in his twinkling dark eyes that said mischief, standing in front of his father who he bore striking similarities to despite the boy's more tanned skin. Beside him, with the woman's hand on his little shoulder was the younger boy who bore an expression like he had seen the worst this world could offer. He carried such grief, such anger and loneliness in those bright blue eyes that Grey felt pity settle in her chest.

As she gazed upon that sad little boy, she noticed something about him that sent chills running down her spine. She'd seen those eyes before; haunting her dreams and wildest fantasies, the eyes she so desperately craved to see. This was the beast and Maksim stood beside him but younger and with less anguish in his stance. Yet under the portrait it read something that left Grey speechless and had her heart pounding fiercely in her chest.

"The Last Volkov Family."

There was a chill that slithered down her spine but it was gone the moment she looked at the names printed below it. And there it was, right after Maksim's name and before 'Lady Volkov', was the name she'd been wondering about since she first took his picture. It was the beast's name, written in strong lettering. Her fingers skimmed over the letters as if to make sure it was real, that she wasn't dreaming this. She'd been so engulfed in the words below the painting to notice the doors creaking open and footsteps approaching her.

"My brother will have your heart hung in this room if he finds you in here."

Grey shrieked and spun around, her hand splayed across her chest as she took in Maksim standing with his arms tucked behind his back, his eyes watching her with a glint of mischief - it was then she saw that little boy staring back at her as him.

"Don't do that to me!" Grey sighed. "I just about pissed myself."

A chuckle left his lips. "Better me than him, aye?"

Grey nodded and turned back to the painting. "These are your parents?"

"Were." He corrected. "I would say good people but that'd be a lie."

Grey turned to him again with a confused expression as he stared at the portrait. He continued, "My father was a terrible man and my mother was the same to anyone but us. She kept it hidden while my father wore his sins on his back."

"What happened to them?"

"Murdered." He looked to the ground with a sigh but he could feel the pity emitting form her. "Don't pity us, Grey, we are not weak. Our parents got what they deserved and one day so will we."

His words left her speechless, the air around them seemed to turn cold. She decided to keep the subject away from the darker parts of the past and instead, Grey pointed to the mystery woman. "Why doesn't your mother have a name?"

"She grew up on the streets of Italy, no family, no parents, she never got a name." He said. "But lord, did she have some amazing stories to tell."

Grey smiled at him. "Can I ask another question?"

"Would me saying no stop you?" He smirked at her and quirked up an eyebrow.

"No." Grey laughed. "Why does the family portrait say 'The Last Volkov Family.'?"

She watched Maksim's face drop and grow cold like his brother's. "Because we are cursed to die alone."

In that stretch of eerie silence was when they heard the front door creak open and slam shut and footsteps echo through the palace, striking fear in both of them. Yet as Grey moved with wide eyes as Maksim ushered her out of the room in a hurry, she felt it - something magical. Something that she could only classify was there by the pounding of her heart and the tingling feeling coming from that mark on her neck. Her body seemed to light up with a form life that had never been experienced before.

And there it was, standing at the end of the hallway with blue eyes swirling with anger. There it was, sizzling in the air as he stormed closer to her, closing the distance between them. There it was drawing her in, leaving her breathless as he was feet away from her. There it was when he grabbed her wrist and yanked her away from Maksim with a vicious growl. There it was all around them, crackling in the air and on their skin like electricity.

There it was: the bond.

Part Sixteen

His long fingers wrapped around her wrist as he pulled her towards him, electricity buzzed in their veins at the contact. It left them both shocked and under any other circumstance, would've rendered them breathless and mesmerized; that was what the bond between two did. It enchanted you. But in the case of a beast, it was anything but magical.

Yet, the electric bond was nowhere near as great as the anger that boiled in that very same blood. "Why were you in there?"

He watched her eyes grow soft yet her jaw was set tightly. She then shrugged and the sass that lingered in her voice only angered him further. "I got bored so I thought I'd explore."

"This hall - that room, is off limits."

"You never said anything of the sort." She snapped back, yanking her wrist free from his grasp and stepping back towards Maksim who watched on carefully.

"Grey." Maksim tried but the girl continued. "Seriously-"

"No! Don't try to act like the good guy, Maksim! Both of you haven't said hardly anything to me at all! You kidnap me and then abandon me?! Last time I checked that's not how it works. And how was I supposed to know you don't want me to explore your home?!" She groaned out. "Do you expect me to live in that tiny room? Bored out of my mind with nothing to do and no one to talk to? To stare out the window and wait for you to come to me like some idiotic damsel?!"

"Grey-"

"No! I am tired! I am so tired of all this bullshit you two have made me go through." She was shaking, both men looking upon her with wary eyes. "I just want to go home."

There was a pause in which both Maksim and Grey turned towards the beast who stood stoic as ever. He simply stared at Grey before he shrugged, his face so blank it gave her the chills. How could someone be so emotionless?

"You can't." He spoke as if it was the simplest thing in the world, as if his words meant nothing at all.

Grey groaned and ran her hands through her hair, moving closer to the beast as she spoke. "If you won't tell me why I can't leave, answer me this; why am I still here? You claimed that your beast 'wanted me', you marked me, yet you leave and hardly even look at me, hell, the only time you dare to touch me is when you're angry at me. So why am I here?"

"Like I said before," He spoke calmly - too calm. "I don't want you, my beast does."

"I don't give a fuck about your beast!" She yelled out. "Just let me go home or kill me! Let my blood paint the walls, I don't fucking care!"

His blank eyes stared at her, a brow raised for a long moment before he decided to ignore her, turning on his heel and walking away from Maksim and Grey.

Maksim put a hand on Grey's shoulder, "Grey-" He spoke but Grey turned to him.

"Fucking leave me alone, Maksim! You're no better than that bastard!"

The fire in her eyes was blazing as she glared at him and with his jaw clenched tight he gave a curt nod and moved quickly down the hall. He passed by his younger brother who had stopped and turned around to look at the human girl with eyes full of rage, not even acknowledging him as he left.

Grey hadn't even noticed his presence still lingered until she spun around after regaining her composure and almost screamed at the sight of him staring at her with those predatory eyes.

"What?" She almost groaned out and looked at him expectantly.

He remained silent, assessing her with those blazing eyes before he spun around and continued to walk. This action angered Grey.

"Tell me the truth." Her voice was calm but on the inside she was raging. He continued to ignore her and started to walk after him with slow steps. "Just tell me the truth, Alexei!"

Everything happened so fast it took Grey a moment to even register what had happened. Her feet were no longer touching the ground and she was shoved against a nearby wall with a hand around her throat, fiery eyes glaring up at her. Her body hung limply before her hands snapped up to claw at his hand that held her throats in a vice-like grip. Her short fingernails did nothing against his smooth skin.

"Where did you hear that name?" He spat, his voice so low it gave Grey the chills. With no answer from her, he repeated it again, this time louder and with a tighter grip on her neck.

She gasped out, trying to let oxygen bless her lungs but nothing came in and no breath came out. Grey was struggling underneath his grip, trying to kick him and claw him with any strength she possessed in this weak state. She was no match against a beast and they both knew this. When his hand loosened its grip just enough for her to breathe, he watched her with a glare as she regained her composure and her breath.

Grey then stared down at him with challenging eyes as she laughed a husky laugh so humorous it almost scared the beast. "Kill me. Do it, I dare you." He snarled at her. "Why don't you do it, Alexei?"

She used his name as a taunt, smirking down at him with such a darkness in her eyes, he froze. "Kill me, Alexei. I have nothing to go back to. I have nothing here. Just put me out of this endless torture. Be kind for once in your life and kill me." Her last words were emphasized by each syllable.

But there it was again, that crackling of electricity in their veins, on their skin and in the air. The bond hit Alexei at full force, almost knocking all the breath from his lungs. It overtook his senses and a moment of weakness struck him as he tried to make sense of what was happening to him. And all that beast inside him needed was a moment.

So as Grey closed her eyes after watching those eyes turn from blue to almost black, she prepared for the death she'd been so greedily awaiting. She craved the sweet release that death would bring, when she'd finally return home and see her mother again. She welcome death with open arms.

But death would never greet her - not yet at least - and as Grey breathed in what she thought was her final breath, it happened.

Her feet touched the ground and the hand that was once on her throat was now holding her waist in a impossibly tight grip while the other was placed on the back of her head. But the most shocking thing of all, the thing that made her eyes shoot open was the feeling of lips upon hers.

Her eyes were only open for just a split second before they were fluttering shut again as she got lost in the kiss. The feeling of the bond and him taking over her. Her hands moved on their own accord, snaking around his broad shoulders to rest one on his back and the other to get tangled in his hair. The kiss was needy, harboring something that could only be described as lust.

In the middle of it all, there was a salty taste that originated from Grey's tear ducts, rolling down her cheeks to where their lips were locked. He pushed against her lips, his body flush against hers, his tongue sliding along her own in every kiss.

A gasp left Grey's lips as he pulled away, looking at her with wide eyes that held something she'd never seen in them before, and quickly disappeared down the same stairs Maksim did what felt like ages ago. With a shaky breath, Grey brought her fingers to her swollen lips that still tingled and buzzed from that electricity between them.

What just happened? She wondered and wondered but nothing that made any sense came to the front of her mind and she was left clueless - and secretly a little turned on - to let her thoughts drive her insane.

With a shake of her head, she wiped away the tears on her cheeks. Hell she'd just received the best kiss of her life but she still cried. Maybe it was due to the fact that she liked it, she liked the way she felt when he touched her and she knew she shouldn't. She knew she should fear him, cower and try to run but it was what she felt deep down that kept her here - not the fear of the cursed forest or the cursed brothers - no, she was here for him, even if she didn't want to be. Fate had already decided it.

She was shaking as she left the hallway and traveled down the stairs and out the front door, grabbing a random coat hung by the door on the way. She was breathing heavily, struggling for air as she stopped outside and stared up at the afternoon sky for a second as if all the answers to her problems would be up in the clouds.

She then looked out at the trees in front of her and decided it best not to travel in there; she didn't want to return inside either so she ventured around the back of the castle. Slowly walking past the side that was ruined and crumbling to the ground, walking past bushes of thorny roses and more tall trees.

Around the back, not much was different aside from the giant, willow tree that leaned a little too far to it's right in front of the forest. A thin layer of frost covered the long tendrils, making them look like beads of crystals dangling from the tree's thick branches. Grey approached the tree with hesitation, her fingers gingerly touching the frozen leaves as if they might break under the slightest bit of pressure. They looked as if they would make music when clinked together by even the softest gust of wind. They looked like something out of a dream.

Moving under the tree, she leaned her back against the trunk and scooted down until the cold snow was against her bottom. She let her head fall back against the trunk, her eyes admiring the melting snowy wonderland, as her long legs stretched out in front of her and she wrapped the coat tighter around her, just now noticing the scent that lingered on it.

She knew it was his.

Alexei.

How the name flowed on her tongue made her shiver and how it seemed to fit him so well. The way he'd reacted when she spoke it, it was if she called him something horrible, but it was just his name. He was no longer the beast, no longer khishchnik to her. No, he was now Alexei, the predator. For no matter what she learned about him, he'd always look at her with those predatory eyes that she could never get out of her head. And now, not only did his eyes haunt her every thought, but his lips still lingered on hers, that tingle still buzzing in her veins. She had thought he hated her, he wanted her blood - he'd said so himself - yet she was still very much alive and breathing and he was over here kissing her. Kissing her and leaving her with feelings she shouldn't have, instead of killing her and burying her in the ground that matched the coldness of her body.

And that seemingly ever-present thought crossed her mind once again: what's happening to me?

Part Seventeen

He watched her from the trees, just sitting under the willow tree until the evening sky turned pink. He watched her as she let her eyes close and her head lay back against the tree's trunk. He watched the steady rise and fall of her chest beneath his coat as she breathed in deeply.

He hadn't the slightest idea as to why he kissed her in the hall, he tried to tell himself it was the beast taking control but it was far too easy to gain control again during the kiss which is unusual. When his beast takes control, it's hell stealing back the reigns. So he knew deep down the kiss was all him with just a little push from that beast inside.

And then there was the way she said his name. Although it was as if she said it to spite him, he wanted to hear her say it again and again. He wanted to hear her whisper it before she fell asleep and when she woke. He wanted to hear her scream it from his bed. He wanted to hear her speak his name as if it was the only word she knew. He'd always despised the name, for it came from the mind of his father, who used to spit it out of his venomous lips as if the sound of the name and sight of his youngest son left him disgusted. He never understood why. Hell, his own brother barely ever called him by name; the only time he had been with it slipping from one's lips was when his mother said it in that voice of hers.

He heard Maksim approach, coming to stand beside him and stare at the human girl out the window. He stayed silent for a long moment, just assessing her from afar before he spoke. "What have you done to her, brother?"

"Nothing."

"When I left, it didn't look like it would escalate into nothing."

"I did nothing, brother." He growled, emphasis lingered on the word 'nothing.' "Leave it."

"I will not leave it because like you something about her draws me in, and unlike you I'd like to see her live."

Alexei turned to Maksim with fierce eyes. "If anything happened to her I'd have an even more insane beast raging inside my head!" His long finger was pressed against his temple for emphasis. "I'd lose my own fucking mind if something happened to her."

"Then why do you constantly threaten her life?!"

"Because I can't decide whether I want her dead or pinned beneath me." The younger brother's words rumbled deep within his chest.

Silence blanketed them for a long moment. "What did you do?" Maksim emphasized every word, looking at his little brother with cold eyes.

Alexei ran his fingers through his hair, looking back at Grey who had moved to pull her legs up to her chest to rest her head upon her knees, hands tangled tightly in her long hair. "I kissed her."

Maksim had expected anything but that. He expected his brother to come home one day with blood staining his teeth, smelling of a sweet human. He had expected to hear of the death of the little boy in the house of the witch. He had seen his brother tear into the flesh of the human boy in the town.

He expected the dark side of his brother, the vicious beast that everyone feared, he grew up around it and had seen it first hand far too many times to count. But not this, never in his life would he have expected to hear his brother kissed someone and ever be this frustrated over it.

Maksim and his brother were not inexperienced when it came to the female species, they were far from it. There was a brothel a few towns over where the women all drooled over the handsome brothers and seemed to throw themselves at them willingly. Each time they'd gone though, which was many a times, never once had he seen his brother look at any of those females with anything but slight disgust, and he had never seen him kiss one. It was his rule, no kissing, just sex. He knew his little brother had never wanted to go but the primal urges inside of him demanding it. The beast inside was unrelenting.

After a long silence, all Maksim managed was a simple: "What?"

• • •

When Grey returned inside after the sun had long since gone away, the sky dark and filled with thousands of bright stars, her cheeks and nose were stained pink. The coat she wore was still wrapped tight around her and she'd expected to be alone - she wanted to be alone for once - but both brothers sat in silence in the living room area. In both theirs hands were small glasses of a clear liquid that could've been considered water but Grey was not dimwitted in any way and she knew it was vodka.

When she entered both their eyes fell upon her yet she found herself staring at Alexei. He stared back with eyes that seemed like they were staring right through her and into her soul. When his eyes left hers to trail down to his coat wrapped around her, she looked away at Maksim who was no longer looking at her but at the bottle of vodka he was using to refill his glass.

"Can I have a glass?"

His head spun around to look at Grey with a confused look. "You drink?"

"Only when I need to forget."

Maksim threw a glance towards his brother who sat in the lonely armchair on the opposite side of the room, staring at the drink in his hand with his other hand gripping the arm of the chair so tight his knuckles were white as the snow outside. He handed Grey a glass as she sat on the long couch in front of the fireplace, between the two brothers but just the slightest bit closer to Alexei. She hadn't noticed it but the beast did, it was rumbling inside his chest at the female he chose.

He watched her with those eyes of his as she stared at the glass she held with shaky hands before she threw it back like a shot, her face contorting in a cringe with the harsh taste. Maksim couldn't fight the smirk tugging at his lips when she held it back out towards him.

"You might want to take it easy." Alexei finally spoke up after her sixth glass when she discarded the coat she wore with a small laugh, throwing it to rest over the couch she was sat on. Grey looked at him with those naturally wide eyes and her cheeks pink from the alcohol and gave him a soft smile.

"I'm fine, beast." She hiccupped in the middle of the final word and Alexei rolled his eyes, Maksim watching on with amusement. "This isn't my first-" Her words broke with another hiccup and she giggled. "-rodeo."

Alexei set his glass on the coffee table and stood, moving towards a curious Grey. He held out his hand for her and she just stared at it for awhile before he grew impatient and gave a small growl as he grabbed her by the bicep and tugged her up. He pulled her out of the room without a word and up the stairs with little struggle.

He made it to her room without a word but she spoke as he opened her door. "Where do you sleep?"

"I don't."

"You don't sleep? Well shit! That's why your so grumpy all the time!" Grey stared up at him as he pulled her towards her bed.

He let go of her and pulled the covers back for her. "Come on. Go to sleep."

Grey opened her mouth to protest but the look he gave her made it snap shut and she pulled the coat she still held up to her chest. He noticed she still had it and cast her an odd glance.

"You know if you take something you're supposed to put it back where you got it." He deadpanned. "The owner might miss it."

Grey shrugged and moved past him to lay on top of her bed, ignoring the covers that had been pulled back. "I like how it smells."

Alexei tensed at hers words and with a final gruff goodnight, he left the room with a beast that needed to be set free far away from her. He moved down the stairs two at a time, trying to get away from the girl as quick as possible but Maksim stopped him at the end of the stairs, he gave his older brother a stern look as he glared at him with his arms crossed.

"The full moon is approaching you know."

Alexei was almost twitching, he couldn't stand still with the beast raging inside of him but his brother wouldn't let him pass. "You think I don't know that?! My control is less and less each fucking day. Now let me pass or else I'm going to march back up those stairs and take her where she lies."

"Don't be stupid." Maksim moved so Alexei could dart past. "I'm tired of cleaning up your messes."

With that, Alexei moved out the front door and into the trees, Grey's words from earlier haunting his head: Only when I need to forget. He was what she wanted to forget. Him and his lips on hers. But he knew even the alcohol couldn't make her forget, and all the bloodshed in the world would never make him forget.

For how could the beast forget the first female, the first human let alone, that could bring him to his knees?

Part Eighteen

Grey's slumber ended before the sun even rose due to the uneasy feeling in her stomach that was shortly after emptied into the toilet. She reemerged from the bathroom after having showered and brushed her teeth three times over, her hair wet and clad in tight leggings and a large T-shirt that had been stuffed deep in the dresser when she first arrived, her thick glasses perched atop her nose.

She looked out the window to see the dark sky slowly turning to a purple, the first signs of the sun peeking over the horizon. Quickly she laced up her boots and tugged on the dark coat she'd woken up beside - even though the scent on it was less, it still smelled of him - before hurrying quietly down the stairs and out towards that willow tree she spent most of last night under. Grey leaned against it and watched the sunshine paint the sky shades of lilac and pink, splashes of orange splattered here and there. She sighed and felt at peace for the first time since arriving in this frozen wonderland.

From one of the higher rooms Grey had yet to explore, he simply watched her, admiring her as she was. After having spent another sleepless night alone, he drowned himself in vodka trying to rid of the emotions growing inside of him towards the girl. He sat outside Grey's door, drinking in her scent like it was his alcohol all night, letting the smell of her tame the beast; and for once in his life, the beast was silent. How he craved to be on the other side of that door, holding her as she slept and maybe, if fate was kind, he'd fall asleep too.

The girl had enchanted him; mind and body. She was a constant thought in his head, a moment to breath in the chaos that was his mind. As much as he didn't want to have the girl around, there was something about her that made everything seem less dark. He knew she felt something for him, she wouldn't have kissed him back or drank last night trying to forget it, and he reveled in that fact. She felt something and with a little push from him the curse could be easily broken but he wasn't sure if he was entirely ready to let someone else see the nightmares in his mind, if he was ready to taint that beauty, to kill the life she held in her eyes.

His past was too dark, too destructive he was afraid as to what would come of the girl once she got a glimpse into who he really was. For even when the curse is broken, the beast inside will vanish but the beast that is him will stay and tear apart her innocence until she is just as hollow and broken as him.

With another large swig of vodka, the bottle is emptied and tossed to the ground where it cracked and rolled against the wall. He glanced at Grey again as her eyes fluttered shut behind those glasses of hers before he turned away from the window and into the room he hadn't inhabited since his mother roamed these halls.

Sitting at the dark stool, he simply stared at the object in front of him before he let his fingers glide over the ivory keys, occasionally touching a black key, ghosting the notes to a song he knew like the back of his hand. As his eyes closed he sucked in a deep breath, releasing it as his fingers played the first notes. Maybe it was the alcohol in his blood, maybe it was just the music, but his body swayed with each note. He'd gotten lost in the music and there was no turning back.

• • •

When Grey returned inside, her ears were lulled by the sounds of a piano coning front upstairs and her nose was assaulted by the sweet swell of syrup. Pushing aside the soft melodies for now, she turned to the kitchen where Maksim was grilling strips of bacon until they were crispy and brown.

"So you're the chef." She said as she sat in one of the island stools, nose wiggling in order to keep her glasses from falling down.

Maksim glanced at her and she noticed his red-rimmed eyes. They were cold, lifeless like they were when they first met. "I may not be great but it's better than raw meat; and it's not often I get to actually make meals."

There was a pause as he filled only two plates with food. Grey spoke quietly. "Are you okay?"

"No." He placed one in front of Grey and the other was set beside her as he perched on the stool and ate in silence.

"Where's your brother?" Maksim's eyes glanced up and she knew he was the one responsible for the music. "Why isn't he eating?"

"Can we please just stop talking about my brother for once and sit in silence?!" Maksim snapped and Grey flinched beside him as he stood up with his plate in his hands and left the room.

Grey finished her meal alone, ignoring her raging thoughts by focusing on the faint piano that never faltered. Not one wrong note, no breaks in the melody. It was a perfect piece only crafted by years of practice. After washing off her plate, she ventured upstairs to retrieve the camera she felt like she hadn't touched in years as well as the cellphone buried at the bottom of her bag. Strapping her camera around her neck and turning on her phone, all hope was crushed when it read 'no service' and she threw it on the ground with a huff.

She left her room, camera pressed against her cheek as she took pictures of every tiny detail in the home. She made her way downstairs, taking her time down there as well as outside before going back into the hallway she was supposedly forbidden from going down. As she walked slowly down the hall, she heard shuffling noises coming from a room she suspected was Maksim's bedroom; making a mental note of which door it was before moving on. She followed the sound of the piano piece that had now turned sad, its notes low and haunting.

She turned the doorknob as slow as she could, cracking the door open quietly, just enough so she could see him. His back was to her, body swaying as his long fingers moved gracefully across each key. She was left breathless as she brought the camera to her cheek and snapped a quick picture of him in this state - looking almost vulnerable. Grey had never seen a beast look so not beastly.

The dim room, along with his dark hair and clothes looked so out of place before the white grand piano, the entire room painted a shade of off-white. It was so elegant and not him.

The music never stopped, even as he spoke. "It's not polite to eavesdrop."

Grey's cheeks flamed red as she quickly turned and was ready to walk away when his voice beckoned her inside.

She paused in her step and turned, pushing the door open and stepping inside, leaving it cracked behind her - afraid to be behind closed doors, alone with him. "I'm sorry. I just-It's hard to ignore such a beautiful melody."

He continued to play until the the song ended with a sinister low note. "Do you play?"

"No, my mother used to though." Grey looked at the camera in her hands as his eyes fell upon her.

"Used to?"

"Yes." She looked up at him and cleared her throat, giving him a tight-lipped smile. "I'm sorry I interrupted."

Grey had her hand on the doorknob when his voice made her freeze. "Why do you avoid me like the plague?"

"Me? Avoiding you?"

"Yes. You drink until all thoughts of me are gone from your mind. You don't look at me anymore." His voice is strained. "You don't have that fire in you anymore."

"That fire has been extinguished with the fear of you." She stared harshly at the door.

She heard the stool scrape against the floor and she spun around to see him standing proudly, broad shoulders back and chin up. "I thought you didn't fear me."

He looked like a proud lion, staring at her from across the room, eyes swirling with something indescribable. "I am afraid of what you do to me."

His eyes darkened, long legs slowly closing the space between them as Grey pressed herself firmly against the door.

"And what do I do to you exactly, Grey?"

She didn't want to answer, but her mouth had a mind of it's own apparently. "You make me feel things I shouldn't feel for a beast."

He was standing in front of her now, chests inches away from touching, breath hot against her nose as he peered down at her with that predatory look. He was waiting for her to speak more but she didn't so he did.

"Do you wish to elaborate?" His head leaned down so his lips moved against her neck and her eyes fluttered shut. "Or am I going to have to pry it from your sweet lips?"

His lips were then locked on her neck, leaving her breathless as he assaulted her skin. "Tell me, lioness. Tell me how I make you feel." Downwards they moved until they were locked around the mark his teeth left in her skin. "Do I make you feel anger? What about excitement? Curiosity or maybe something deeper?" His hands trailed down her sides until they were on her ass, pressing her against him firmly.

She left out a shaky breath as he rocked against her, teeth against her mark nibbling lightly. "Do you lust after me like I do you? Do I haunt your dreams like you haunt my every waking moment?"

Grey found her voice, hands going to his shoulders in an attempt to push him away but the bond was too strong it made her arms weak. "Stop."

"What if I don't want to?"

She was biting back a moan from the feel of his hands massaging her bottom. As much as she was fighting it, he was stronger than her and she found herself in the air, her legs forced to wrap around his waist. His grip on her bottom was still firm, holding her against him so she could feel how much he wanted her as his lips continued to assault the mark.

"Alexei-"

A growl shook his chest. "Say it again."

She shivered as his lips moved away from the mark and across her jaw. "No. Stop this."

His lips were on the corner of her own, teasing her. "Make me."

Grey grew frustrated, whether it be from Alexei's constant teasing or the fact that she wanted him and wanted to push him away at the same. With a groan she placed her hands on his chest - trying her hardest to ignore the heat coming off his hard chest - and gave a weak attempt at pushing him off.

His chuckle was dark against her neck. "You're going to have to try harder than that lioness. My beast is out and he wants a taste." After his final word, his tongue left a wet, hot line up her neck from her collarbones to her jaw, making her suck in a sharp, shaky breath.

That's when Grey broke, lost all control and she began to weep as she placed her hands on his cheeks and yanked his lips to hers, kissing him so fiercely he was shocked. He kissed her back, just as passionately for a few moments before he pulled away and placed her on the ground so his hands could cup her cheeks, staring at her with an emotion swirling in those blue eyes Grey had never seen in him before. Worry.

"Why are you crying?"

Grey pushed herself away from him, away from the wall so she could breath as she stood before the grand piano wiping away her tears. "I don't know. Everything is just so-so confusing!"

"Why?"

"I shouldn't be feeling what I feel for you. I hardly know you but I let things like this happen between us." Grey ran a hand through her hair and in an attempt to change the conversation away from her emotions, she looked at Alexei. "Does Maksim hate you?"

He tensed. "Why would you ask that?"

"He snapped at me this morning when I asked about you."

He seemed to let out a breath full of relief. "Today's not the best day to talk to him."

"Why?"

"Why does it matter?"

"Because I consider him a friend." Grey mustered up a glare towards Alexei who cocked up one eyebrow. "I actually care about him."

Back was the beast; cold and sarcastic. "Why don't you ask him yourself then?"

"Because he obviously doesn't wish to talk."

"Sounds like a you problem." Alexei shrugged and Grey screamed out in frustration.

"Just tell me what is wrong with him asshole!"

Grey watched his eyes darken, jaw grow tight with anger and his fists clench. "Watch your tongue."

"Watch where you put your tongue." She threw back, crossing her arms over her chest and sitting into one hip. Just when she thought they were getting somewhere, everything was ruined.

After a long silence, Grey huffed. "If you're going to be an-"

"Today's the anniversary of the death of our mother."

Part Nineteen

Grey was frozen, staring at Alexei who watched her with those lifeless eyes. She didn't know how to react, she was conflicted with wanting to hug Alexei and tell him she's sorry or run away. After a few moments of watching her, Alexei backed away and she frowned at him.

"I see the pity in your eyes." He almost snarled. "I don't need it."

"Ale-"

"No. I don't need your condolences or any form of sympathy from you or anyone. I am not weak."

With that his back is turned to her and he begins to leave the room, but not without one final demand:

"I've told you before this hall is forbidden. Do not let me catch you in here again."

Alexei was down the stairs and moving away from her tantalizing scent as quick as he could go. He couldn't handle it, that look she was giving him. He didn't want to feel the pain of losing his parents again; he didn't want to be weak. He was taught at a young age that weakness is even the most powerful man's downfall. He wanted to lose himself, his thoughts, his feelings to the familiar haze that only vodka could bring to him, and after he'd drank the cabinets dry, he'd let the beast out on the world.

Upon entering the kitchen, he found Maksim perched atop a bar stool with a glass of dark liquid; whiskey, his favorite. It was the brothers' tradition each year on the day of their mother's death to drink up all the liquor in the cabinet until the sky was dark and become the beasts they are to roam the night. Alexei had just missed part of the beginning.

With a bottle of vodka in his fingers, he sat beside his older brother and clicked the bottle to the glass before tossing it back and taking big gulps.

"Why are you not with her?" Maksim's eyes never left his drink.

"This is our time - tradition, brother."

"Not for long." The glass was emptied between Maksim's lips and he looked to his little brother. "She will become your new tradition and I'll be left here to drink myself to death."

"I won't abandon you; I owe you everything."

Maksim's voice grows quiet as he pours himself another glass. "I would've given up everything for Emilie."

"You loved her."

"And you'll soon learn to love Grey like I loved her." Maksim held up his glass. "Cheers brother. May mother's legacy never die."

As the brothers downed their drinks, Grey entered the kitchen and both their eyes were drawn to her. She stood there and stared at them, eyebrows knotted together in thought as she bit her bottom lip. The younger brother was restless at the sight of her so he stood sharply and was out of the home in an instant with a low growl.

Grey stared after him for a minute before turning to Maksim who had a brow perked up as he looked at her. "It's quite late, you should rest."

Maksim snorted. "Don't act like you care about our wellbeing, Grey. Our deaths would be the happiest moment of your life."

"I wouldn't wish that upon you. . . or even the beast."

"Shouldn't you be asleep?" He retorted and she shrugged. "After I finish the bottle I'll be stumbling to bed."

"What about Alexei?"

"He doesn't sleep much," he said. "Never has."

"Why?" Grey looked back where the beast had disappeared awhile ago as if he'd come storming back for her using his name.

"It's the curse. As a child he had insomnia a lot, our mother would give up her sleep to just lay with him and sing to him until he fell asleep. When he got old enough for the curse to finally settle, it got worse and he was plagued with nightmares. He'd scream in his sleep and when we'd go to try to wake him, he'd attack us." Maksim shrugged. "He never told us what he saw when he slept but every time he finally woke up it'd look like he just saw himself die a thousand times over."

"That's terrible."

He shrugged and gulped down more of his drink. "None of us got much sleep back then, that's why he stopped sleeping every night. He felt guilty. I started having nightmares too, still get 'em sometimes. Everything would just be black and I'd hear his scream, that scream was haunting. It wasn't like he was afraid, but more like he was being torn apart from the inside out and I never understood; still don't." Maksim met Grey's gaze, silver eyes filled with sadness. "He's got it worse than me or anything else in this forest. You can't blame him for the terrible things he does, he can't stop them."

"Your mother and him, they were close?"

"He was her malen'kiy volk. Her little wolf." Maksim downed the rest of his rest. "He takes today the hardest, leave him be until he comes to you."

"If he doesn't?"

"He will. He'll always come back for you."

• • •

Petra stared out at the trees from her usual perch on Grey's back porch. Her grandmother had come by with Rosalie on her hip who reached her little hands out for Petra but she didn't even glance at the little girl. Klara expressed her worry towards her granddaughter but the girl had this hollow look in her eyes that always seemed to stray away and glaze over. She always seemed to be anywhere but where she actually was.

She was waiting for the day khishchnik walked out of those trees; the day she'd kill him. She wanted to avenge her friend, she didn't know whether Grey was alive or dead but she did know that she would be the one to end the reign of terror that beast brought upon the town.

Whenever Petra was little and her mother often told her the story of the predator of their town, she knew that there were some truths but she never fully believed it until Grey disappeared.

The story told of an angry man, a man without any sort of remorse. A man of endless wealth who committed such an unspeakable crime, he was cursed by a witch to live out his days alone. His personality was already horrid, she just needed to make him so ugly on the outside, he'd never find true happiness. So she made him a lycan. The witch told him the only way to rid of the beast was to have a woman love him and he love her back just as fiercely; she did this because she knew the chances of him breaking it were slim to none. A monster of a human and a beast of a lycan; who could love that? Yet, despite his infliction, he found a woman and made her his wife, thinking their undying love would break the curse but they were too corrupt. They were two dark souls, made for one another in the deepest pits of hell. The witch knew this from the minute he laid his beady eyes on the woman, who from the outside, carried herself with the utmost elegance and innocence. But behind that smirk of hers, was darkness. So much darkness.

When their first son came, the witch was ready to curse him as well, but she saw that he already carried the curse in his blood thanks to his father. He was the first born son, he was already destined for a rough life. The beast still raged inside of the man and he did everything he could to rid of it before his wife fell pregnant with another child. And he thought he had gotten rid of the curse for awhile.Then came the second son, the stillborn who's first breath was thanks to the witch's spells. The night he was born, the beast returned through the man and he blamed the second son for it. He blamed the curse returning on him, for having to seek out the witch to make his son breathe. The witch almost felt sorry for the youngest boy, who - as he grew older - wore the curse on his back in the form of licks from his father's whip. She saw their futures in their baby blue eyes and just about wept for the boys. What had she done? She asked herself this question until she lay on her deathbed, wishing she could reverse the curse but it was too late and the boys had already grown old and left a trail of bodies in their pasts.

The story then went on to tell of a day when the brothers would emerge from the trees with a girl on one of their arms and they'd be free from the curse. But even if the curse was broken, it could never take away the darkness that was passed down from their parents, nor the darkness they had brought upon themselves. They'd bore too many sins to become good even after the curse is broken.

"When are you going to give up?" Dimitri's voice was behind her but her eyes never strayed from the trees.

"Never."

"Petra. She's not coming back." His voice was strained, he was sad too, she knew he missed Grey but he was so quick to give up all hope. "She's probably-"

Petra whipped around, her eyes finding something other than trees for the first time in days. "Don't you dare say it! I know she's out there and I know she wants to go home! She's never going to love that monster."

"How do you know? How can you be so sure that she's not dead or that she isn't in love with one of them?" Dimitri was almost as furious as the shaking Petra.

"He killed your family, Dimitri! He killed Ethen and he almost killed you." Petra shook her head at him. "Why defend him when you know he's a beast better than anyone else? I know that once Grey figures out all that he's done she'll never love him."

"What about the brother? Maksim? What darkness does he carry to scare her away?"

"She's already bonded with khishchnik. The bond is only broken by death you know this."

"But if theirs isn't acted upon what's to say Maksim won't take her like he took the last girl?"

Petra paused. "Dimitri-"

"She may not be dead now, but I promise you they will kill her just like they killed her." His voice was dark. "When that day comes, I hope I'm far from here so the last memories I have of Grey are her alive and not her shell of a body."

Petra stared at the boy for a moment before realizing how his eyes were underlined with dark circles and there was a slight shade along his jawline. He looked like he'd been through hell and back yet oddly enough, he looked like a man.

"Where are you going?" She spoke softly, her heart breaking more than it already had.

"I'm leaving for America in the morning. I can't be here anymore, I can't deal with the cursed forest or Grey's disappearance. It's just too much."

"Can you do me a favor when you get there?" He nodded as she wrapped her arms around him and hugged him. "Find Grey's family and make sure they know she's alright, no one can know she's vanished."

"And what if you don't find her? If you do and she's. . ."

"I'll contact her family myself." Petra stared at Dimitri with such passion in her eyes it left him breathless. "Be safe my brother."

"Be safe my sister." Dimitri bowed the slightest to the girl who smiled. "Don't be foolish."

{in case y'all didn't catch on dimitri and petra aren't blood related, they just took him in and raised him as their own after his parents}

Part Twenty

{ i'm so in love with this song right now it's so pretty.M xx}

Grey's night was long and sleepless. Spent staring out the window of her room, counting the stars and watching the brothers run through the trees. She heard their howls, mournful, sweet melodies that stirred the creatures of the night. For this one night, they were not beasts, they were not seeking blood, they crave the taste of the sweet liquid that dropped from human veins, nor the bitter scent of death lingering in the air. No, they were broken souls this night. And Grey heard this in their songs to the almost full moon, she saw it in Maksim's eyes the next afternoon, she could feel it in the air; they missed their mother with every fiber of their beings.

"Maksim?" Grey was cautious as he set a plate down in front of her. "I'm sorry."

His eyes met hers. "It's the past."

"But it's not. It may have happened years ago but it's still a part of you. It's not okay to push it down, to act like it doesn't effect you both the way it does. . ."

He was silent for awhile and Grey would've thought he had left had she not been looking at him. He shook his head and shrugged. "She wouldn't have wanted us to mourn her like this. But it's hard no to when it's been eighteen years."

"How old were you?"

"Ten. Alexei had just turned eight."

Grey was left speechless. The human girl knew loss, she knew it all too well, she knew what if felt like to lose your mother, but to have been through so much at a young age, she couldn't imagine what they must of felt. And she didn't even want to imagine what events happened afterwards that made them who they were now. As she opened her mouth to speak, in walked the beast himself with his shoulders back and head high, his stoic face and snarky attitude back as if yesterday never happened.

The moment he entered, Maksim's head whipped towards him, eyes ablaze and nostrils flaring, but Alexei was only focused on Grey.

She couldn't help but take him in as he did her - almost as if it was natural - he looked more confident, stronger, there was something different in the air around him that had Grey breathing in through her nose and out of her mouth in an attempt to calm her racing heart. It didn't work.

Maksim stood and took a stance in front of Grey which Alexei did not take kindly to. This male, brother or not, was too close to his female. He greeted his older brother with a growl of warning, sharp teeth bared in a threat.

"I thought we agreed you'd stay far away today, brother." Maksim's voice was harsh, an underlying hint of annoyance masked in venom.

Alexei's vicious demeanor dropped and instead he gave a casual shrug and walked towards where lunch lay on the counter. "The day is young and nightfall is nowhere near."

"The moon is high in the midnight sky somewhere. You are not stable today and I thought we agreed you'd stay away."

He shrugged again and leaned against the counter as he chewed a piece of his sandwich. Once again, his predatory eyes were on Grey and hers were on him.

"What's going on?" She finally asked.

"The full moon is tonight." Maksim said, sitting down slowly with his eyes still on his brother.

"And?"

"The moon brings out the darkest beasts, little lion." Alexei said. "And my beast wants out to play with you." He snapped his teeth at her in order to get a reaction, and he got just that.

A shiver passed through her body, not going unnoticed by Alexei who's eyes grew dark as he watched her reaction to him. His hands tightened on his plate, his restraint slipping.

Maksim growled. "Watch yourself, brother."

"I'm fine." Alexei's voice was gravelly, growling out his words through clenched teeth.

Maksim turned to Grey slowly, his body angled enough to where he could still see his brother. "I think it's best if you go upstairs and lock yourself in your room. I would like to end my night with a nice glass of whiskey, not cleaning up the dead."

With wide eyes and a nod, Grey left her lunch on the island half finished and began to walk out of the room, her eyes lingering on Alexei for as long as they could.

He watched her walk out until she was completely out of view, but the image of her hips swaying slightly with each step she took would be forever burned into his mind. It was barely past noon but his beast was pacing inside of him already, anticipating nightfall and being able to roam with full control.

Alexei knew the beast's intentions for when the moon was high in the sky. He knew he wanted Grey, plain and simple. He was raging inside, wanting out to get a taste of her not only her sweet body, but her blood too. However, he didn't know the full extent of what that beast would do to get her.

"I'm restraining you earlier tonight." Maksim stated calmly as he washed the plates. "You've never had a bond with a full moon and I fear for not only her life but yours, brother."

"Double up on the chains and locks." Alexei was looking at his older brother with pained eyes. "Do whatever you can to not let me out. He wants her and he won't stop for anything until he has her."

Maksim's deep breath was the only sign he was still listening. He turned around, facing Alexei and he nodded. "I will do everything I can but we both know tonight will be just the beginning of a whole new hell."

Had Maksim not been listening he wouldn't have caught his brother's soft words. "Don't let me hurt her."

"You have my word." He breathed out slowly. "Go find some way to calm the beast for now. Go far away. I have to go speak with Grey."

Maksim was leaving the kitchen before Alexei could answer, he couldn't handle it in there another minute. He'd never seen his brother like that, not even when their mother died. Never had he seen him look so torn. Never had he seen him look so weak yet so strong. It scared him just the slightest.

Walking up the stairs to Grey's room, Maksim's mind was plagued with worry of what the moon would bring tonight. He worried more about his brother than Grey - she was tough, she could overcome anything that happened tonight - because God knows that if something happened to her tonight, Alexei would never forgive himself and he would never admit that it hurt him. He never liked being seen as weak, it was something their father had programmed into his mind at such a young age. Even as their father would punish him in the most cruel ways, Alexei wouldn't make any sign that it hurt because if he did, he'd get a whole new round of torture.

Grey opened the door immediately after he knocked, it was as if she was waiting for him. Her wet hair and overwhelming scent of lavender filling her room showed him that she'd just finished showering. She looked at him in question, begging for answers to all the questions that plagued her mind. And how he wished he could answer all her questions and send her back home. The poor girl didn't deserve this life, she deserved so much more but fate was cruel to even the kindest of souls.

"Maksim?" Her voice held fear of the unknown.

"I need you to understand that we are cursed, we were not meant to be beasts, we were meant to be human. Our father is the reason we are what we are and as you can tell Alexei has the worst of it. He would've been just a normal lycan, but our father wasn't a good man and he was full of hatred. All that hate and darkness made the curse worse." Maksim entered the room and paced as Grey sat on her bed. "When Alexei was born he lacked a heartbeat and our father may have been a terrible man but he loved our mother and seeing her break as she looked at Alexei drove him off the edge. He sought the help of the only witch he knew - the witch who cursed him - and he managed to make a deal with her to bring Alexei back. What our parents hadn't known was that our father had broke the curse long ago and when he needed the witch's help, she made him a beast again without his knowledge. When she brought Alexei back to life, she cursed him as well in the process; she never meant to do it but she did."

"Our father blamed Alexei for his affliction and took out all his rage on him from the time he could walk. Mother would always try to stop him, try to protect her baby boy but he'd always win and Alexei would end up with lash marks down his back. I always watched on from inside, I wanted to help but what could I do against my own father? I watched my little brother suffer and my mother cry as she tended his wounds and I never did anything about it. I'd still listen to my father teach me how to be a man, how to be a human who was feared by all."

"Human? But-"

"I was never cursed. When my mother got pregnant with me, my father still carried the lycan gene and it was passed down to me. So no matter what happens, I will always have the wolf inside of me."

"Wait - So if the curse is broken, Alexei will be human and you'll still be a lycan?" Maksim nodded. "Does he know?"

"If he knew he'd never try to break the curse, he'd let himself suffer just so I wouldn't be alone. He'd die for me."

"He's kind."

"He's foolish."

"Did your father know?" Grey was about ready to cry, these poor brothers.

"I didn't figure out until I shifted for the first time long after my parents died. I thought I was cursed too until I realized what happens to Alexei every full moon happened to my father and not me or any other born lycan."

Maksim sighed. "I'm stuck like this but I have learned to live with it. I'm tired of having to chain my brother up in the forest every full moon." He looked at Grey with such an intensity it left her breathless. "Please Grey, help me free him."

• • •

By the time Maksim joined him in the forest, the sun had painted the evening sky orange and red. In his gloved hands he carried large silver chains that Alexei would be adorning on this eerie night.

"How is she?" Was all that he asked.

"She is locked in her room with a dresser in front of her door. The front door is locked tight, as well as all the windows." Maksim spoke as he wrapped the chains around a thick tree.

Alexei stood and watched the sun slowly disappear beneath the horizon, his thoughts only on Grey, he was staring at the sky, praying to whatever higher power looked down at him to not let him harm the human girl. Begging the night to pass without her bloodshed.

When he turned back to Maksim, he was watching him with sad eyes. "I hate doing this to you."

"It's for the best."

He sighed as he stripped of all of his clothes, discarding them on the ground before him. Thankfully, now that almost all of the snow had disappeared from the ground, it was warmer and smelled of spring and summer. He let Maksim bind his wrists and ankles, the worst one going around his neck; he'd no doubt have marks in the morning.

And as the final rays of sunlight left the sky to the moon, Alexei felt his body begin to change, more painful than all the other times. His screams and grunts of pain made Maksim cringe as he watched on from a distance. His pleas to his brother to let him free, that the silver was burning. His begging to the moon to stop all this and free him from a life of misery. This part was always the worst for Maksim and Alexei; the elder watching his brother wish for death was something no sibling should ever witness of their family. Then it was all silenced when that auburn beast finally stood on four legs in front of that tree. Chains tight around it's legs and neck, panting heavy as its head was tilted down to the ground.

Even though Alexei and his beast were far different creatures, it's mind was still filled with the silver eyes and endless legs of Grey. Everything that drew not only the beast, but the human as well, to her. It breathed in deeply and even though they were miles away, that lavender scent filled it's veins and drove it mad.

Maksim knew it was going to be a long night when the beast looked up and it's eyes were shining blue.

Part Twenty One

Everything was silent in the house, so silent that Grey didn't even want to breathe in fear that she might breathe too loud. She had her back against the wall opposite of the door with the dresser in front of it, the knife Maksim gave her sat on the nightstand only a few feet away. Her eyes never strayed from that door, no matter how badly she wished to look out the window, she was terrified, her body frozen in fear.

Truly, deeply terrified of what lurked outside. She knew that the moon didn't bring any good when it hung full and ominous in the night sky. And after all that Maksim had told her she was left alone and shaking, unable to will her body to hold that beautiful knife that could save her life.

"If he somehow breaks free and comes here. Do not hesitate to stab him. Get his arm, his leg, anywhere to make him immobile, but if you have to kill him. Do it."

She knew that if it came down to it, her or him, she'd never be able to kill him even if he was a beast. She would let the beast tear her throats out and feast on her guts as long as Alexei would live. Why she'd give her own life before his was beyond her, but she just knew she would.

Out of the silent night, broke a wild, feral howl that seemed to shake the entire earth. It sounded far away but Grey knew those creatures were fast and powerful and they could be near her in no time. She watched the digital numbers of her beside clock turn to a hour after midnight, and out of nowhere it came; that bond. It crept through her veins and coiled around her lungs, she felt like she was drowning as the urge to find him, see him, touch him overwhelmed her entire being. It was taking over her senses and any sense she had left was swept from her mind as if common sense was useless. And yet, despite her better judgment, she crawled over to the window, slow and quiet, and squatted down low so she could peek out the window without being fully seen.

Outside, the world seemed peaceful and beautiful. The world now turning green was filled with fireflies, where she usually watched little creatures scurry across the grass there was nothing. Everything seemed out of place except for those fireflies floating around the trees. The outside world called out to her. She could see the wind rustling the tall tree and if her window had been open, she was sure she would've heard that eerie little voice beckoning her into the trees. Her finger twitched with the urge to pull her window open and breath in the night air or even to creep down the stairs and step into the world illuminated by moonlight. Grey had been so entranced by the seemingly magical world, that she hadn't noticed she was no longer crouching but standing at her full height, peering out the window. Her wide eyes scanned the tall trees that swayed in greeting, begging her to come to them, but the only thing that planted her feet in their place and kept her inside that room, were the big blue eyes peering from behind the lights of the fireflies.

And she was mesmerized, it was like seeing them again for the first time. Frozen in her spot high above the beast, she watched it slowly emerge from the trees. The beast seemed larger than normal, it's legs thicker with muscle and teeth sharper, with each step it took she could see the muscles ripple beneath its shining fur. It was far more intimidating as it made it's presence know in the night that now lacked that magic vibe with the fireflies gone and trees still and sinister looking again.

As it looked up at her and she looked down at it, Grey felt her heart drop when she realized that it's huge claws and teeth were stained with blood.

Maksim.

The spell broke between their locked gazes and she fell down as her legs gave out, her body sprawled across the ground, chest heaving with fear. As quick as she could, she scurried over the door, pulling herself up so she could press an ear to it, trying to listen for any signs that could indicate there was any more danger than that which she was already in.

With her ear pressed firmly to the door, the knife that glistened in the dark was in her direct line of sight. It taunted her. It's silver blade and handle that was carved with designs that matched the big doors that hid the room filled with generations of portraits. She knew she'd need it if he got inside but right now, it was only her in the house and she wouldn't dare touch it until-

The long scratches at the front door were sinister and she froze before the whines filled with false innocence followed and made goosebumps rise on her skin. He wanted in. He wanted her. He kept at that pattern, scratching and whining for what felt like hours before it all got silent and was replaced by a menacing growl. Grey froze, a shiver ripping down her spine.

Yet despite her fear of what would happen if he got in, she could only think of Maksim. Where is he? Is he okay? Is he alive? Her thoughts were running rampant, forgetting about the situation at hand. She didn't hear the silence that followed the growl, nor the growls that rumbled through him as he move around the castle, therefore Grey didn't hear the sound a downstairs window shattering.

She froze again when a low growl tore through the silent air, the beast's claws clicking on the linoleum echoed upstairs. Her heart dropped; that meant the beast was inside.

He was coming for her.

Moving as fast as she could she ran to the window in her room, but not without grabbing that silver knife first. With a hard pull the window slid open and Grey had one leg dangling out of it when her door rattled. She froze in her place, unable to will herself to move. The door shook as the beast threw all it's might against it. She watched the cracks grow up the wooden door, creating thick, jagged lines that signaled her demise.

Throwing her other leg over she looked down at the ground below. It's only two stories. She told herself she'd be fine, she could handle a fracture in her leg or foot but a beast she could not. Throwing that silver knife down first, far enough to the side that she wouldn't fall on it and impale herself, she took in a deep breath. And as the door burst open and the beast walked in, Grey was giving the final push off as she hurdled towards the ground.

Her own scream covered the sound of the beast's angry growls as he peered down at Grey who lay on the ground coughing and gasping for breath. She sobbed as she pushed herself up and onto aching legs to reach the knife and run. No broken bones (that she knew of) but her previously injured ankle was throbbing beneath her weight. With the knife gripped tightly in her hand, she took in a final deep, shaky breath before she took off into the forest as quick as her recently injured legs could carry her.

The beast's growls ripped through the air around her as she ran through the dark trees. Where she was going was beyond her; maybe she was going home, maybe she was looking for Maksim, maybe she wanted the beast to chase her. Anywhere, even the cursed trees seemed better than a beast that lusted after her body and blood.

Grey kept running and she didn't dare to stop for anything. She knew she was lost but she didn't care, she was determined to keep running until daylight.

But that was soon broken.

When she broke through the tree line, she realized the trees had moved. They had done their sick job, and Grey was somehow facing the side of the little castle that was in ruins. She froze and stood there, shaking her head in disbelief. She was not back here. She began to hyperventilate as she looked around before darting back into the trees. They can't trick her.

Running and running and running. Grey's legs burned and ached, her lungs were struggling to pull in air, she was even crying but she didn't falter in her pace. She just wanted the sun to rise so she could tell an alive Maksim that she was going home and that she was sorry for abandoning them. She missed New York and its civilization, where no beasts chased her through haunted trees.

But as she was preparing herself for daylight, she found him in the night-time. She almost tripped over something large but thankfully caught herself and happened to look down. Grey tensed up as she looked down at a bloodied Maksim.

Her hand came up to cover her mouth as she sobbed, collapsing next to him. Her hands moved to grab his hand when she noticed his shallow breathing and she moved one hand off of his and onto his bruised cheek.

"Maksim, what has he done to you?" Her voice was soft, tears streaming down her cheeks as she took in his form. The gashes down his side, chunks of skin missing surrounded by teeth marks, they were slowly healing and closing but they still looked brutal. She could tell the beast hadn't desired to kill him, but it had come so close.

"I did what I had to do."

The voice echoed around her, making her jump to her feet and spin around in search of the owner. She knew his voice, of course, it was burned in her brain, and now as it bounced of the trees it carried something different in the tone. Something darker that made his voice drop a few octaves. He was hidden in the trees again, just like the first few times they met and she felt like his prey all over again.

"You almost killed your brother." Grey spat, taking a protective stance by Maksim and not letting her fear show despite her shaking hand that held the knife tightly.

"He wouldn't have let me get to you otherwise." His voice was behind her, his breath on her hair.

Grey spun around but no one was there. "You could've waited until morning to find me."

"Now where's the fun in that?" He hummed a low chuckle. "I like this game we've got going on, and now that the moon's out it's so much better."

Grey's eyes were darting around, searching for his figure in the darkness. "What game?"

"I haven't figured out a name yet but you should know the rules. You've played it far better than I."

"The only one playing games here is you, Alexei."

His growl filled the air and the next thing she knew, Grey was pulled away from Maksim's body, her back was pulled against a hard chest, thick arms wrapping around her torso. She gasped as the bond buzzed in her veins with the feel of this man - this beast - pressed against her. Her hair was fisted on one side in his large hand and he tugged her head to said side, exposing the side of her neck with his mark to him. Her own fingers were digging into the skin on his forearms in an attempt to pry him off her.

His lips brushed the mark on her neck with each word he spoke. "You've been playing the greatest game of all, Grey." She shivered as he whispered her name. "You pretend to loathe me, to fear me, to hate me but I know you don't. I know you dream of me at night. I know you ask Maksim about his past and mine. I know you want me just as much as I want you. I usually enjoy a good game of chase to tease my prey but I'm quite bored of chasing you and I want you now."

And when his lips were locked on her neck, Grey knew she was done for. There was no going back now.

~~~

HERE IS THE DESCRIPTION OF MY NEXT BOOK: ATLAS(if y'all want more as in a prologue lmk i'll give it to you lovely people)

Atlas Reign was a lab experiment. She couldn't remember what the world outside of the colorless walls of the facility looked like; it'd been too long. She'd been taken by the government after the exploitation of her species, they wanted to know what made the lycans tick and how to defeat them and that's why they had Atlas.

Day after day they broke her, experimenting on her in the worst ways imaginable, bringing her to the brink of death before pulling her back to life, torturing her and the wolf inside of her until it was gone.

And just when Atlas was ready to give up, His pack was there to pull her out of her hell.
~~~

Part Twenty Two

There she was. She had burst through the trees with the same aura she always bounced into the rooms with despite this horrible night. Her eyes landed on him, back leaned against a tree with his legs stretched in front of him, hand covering a bloody gash on his stomach. She paused, that peaceful and happy air around her gone and in its place was despair. He watched her approach him with her big teary eyes.

"Maksim." That honey sweet voice filled his ears and all his pain was gone with just her voice. "What has he done to you, my love?"

He could hear Grey's voice mixing in with his unconscious memories, her voice was far away as she called out his name frantically. He could feel a hand holding his own, resting on his cheek, but he couldn't tell who was touching him or whether it was real or not. He tried to move, tried to yell but his body was paralyzed with pain. In and out he drifted into the land of dreams and reality.

"Maksim, come on baby." He hadn't heard her voice in years, it encouraged him to focus on his memories that now seemed like dreams. He faded far away from Grey and came to her.

"Emilie?"

He opened his eyes and everything was hazy. Nothing but the morning sky was visible through the morning mist. He swore he had heard her voice but no one was there. He blinked a few times but the haze wouldn't go away around the edges of his vision, so with shaky, weak arms he pushed himself up to sit.

And there was Alexei, looking at him as if he'd seen a ghost. His eyes were wide and his mouth stuttered as if he wanted to speak. Blood coated his fingertips up to his forearms and he shook violently. He had just shifted back, Maksim could tell by the way his wolf's pelt lay on the ground not far away.

"Alexei?"

"I'm so sorry."

Maksim frowned. "What?"

"I should've stopped him. I should've tried to stop him but I just watched him do it." Alexei looked absolutely insane. "He was too strong. The moon was so full and the pull was too strong. I couldn't stop him-I didn't even try, brother. I'm so sorry."

"What are you talking about?"

Alexei froze, his hand slowly moving into the air as he pointed a shaky red finger to the left of his brother. Turning his head slowly in the direction he pointed, Maksim felt his heart stop.

Scrambling over to her, he forgot his own wounds as he muttered denials under his breath and gathered her limp body into his arms. The first thing he noticed was how cold she was, her skin no longer glowed with warmth and instead it looked dull and ghostly pale under the morning light. He didn't even feel the sparks like he did just hours before. Her eyes were closed, mouth parted, she looked like she was asleep and Maksim would've thought that, had a chunk of her throat not been missing. Scratches littered her body from his brother's claws but that bite to her neck had been the finishing moving. Emilie was dead. She was dead and it was all Alexei's fault.

• • •

His hands were everywhere. They left a scorching trail of heat up and down Grey's sides and even down to the back pockets of her jeans where his dangerous hands seemed to linger the most. She knew he was still a beast even if he looked like a human seeing as though the moon still hung high in the sky, but everything he was doing felt so right. She could feel how much he wanted her and she was somewhat relieved that he wanted her just as much as she did him.

Grey suddenly pulled away, holding his face in place by placing firm hands on his cheeks, closing her eyes and resting her forehead against his. She took a few moments to calm her racing heart by breathing in deep and slow. She was still clouded with lust towards this beast of a man.

"Alexei." She spoke softly. "Come back to me. Don't let him win."

A growl rumbled in the beast's chest and Grey watched a bone in his arm snap, claws replacing his fingernails. He was going full beast again and who knew what this beast would do to her with complete control.

Alexei could feel his control slipping. The beast was raging, it didn't want Grey to want his human side, only the beast. He wanted her to crave the beast side, he wanted to show her who she really wanted by filling the night with her moans. Alexei wouldn't let that happen, what with his emotions slowly turning into the beast's.

"Grey." Alexei groaned out, claws digging into her skin as his hip bone cracked.

"I'm here. Don't leave me Alexei." Her voice shook; she was terrified but she was a lioness who never admitted to that fear. "Don't let him take over. He hurt Maksim. He hurts people, not you."

A snarl tore through Alexei's throat as more bones broke and the beast grew closer to the surface. He was so focused on pushing down the beast and his own pain that he didn't recognize Grey's when she winced and tightened her grip on his face with her jaw clenched tight.

"I want you, Alexei, not the beast."

"I am the beast." He just about sobbed out as he squeezed his eyes shut.

"You don't kill for pleasure-"

"I let him."

And Grey's voice was drowned out by a cry of pain from Alexei that he didn't even hear her soft words.

"I can't love a beast."

Alexei felt the change begging to take over completely, that itching feeling of fur growing beneath his skin took over and in an attempt to scratch it away, his skin came with it. He stared at the bloodied fur on his shoulder before turning up to Grey who stood watching him, clutching her bloody hips. It was then that Alexei noticed the claw marks on her hips from his grip, the ground by her feet stained with her blood that trailed down her long legs. He hurt her; and for some reason, that hurt him - the human side of him at least.

"Get out of here Grey." His voice broke as he winced.

"But, Alexei-"

"I don't want to hurt you more! Leave! Go West-" He paused to breath as more bones broke and re-shifted, his finger pointing in the direction he spoke of. "You'll find Petra and the town there. Go back to New York."

Grey shook her head. "No. I'm not leaving you."

"You will leave me." Alexei looked at her, pleading with his eyes. "I won't be able to live with myself if I hurt you."

"It's not you!"

"I am one with this beast. I am as much a part of khishchnik as he is a part of me! Go!"

Grey grew angry, her hands moved to hold his cheeks as he cried out in pain again. She looked into his eyes, his human eyes as his body was halfway between man and beast. "I know there is good inside of you, Alexei. Don't let the darkness win."

He stared back at her, his body calming enough for Grey to think he won, that the beast was tamed but the snapping of his jaw beneath her palms made her stomach churn.

"Grey. Go!"

It took everything in her to not stay with him as he screamed and groaned through his shift. To force her legs to move was hard enough but making them run and not stop was draining her from just a few feet. Grey continued straight forward in the direction Alexei pointed, never once faltering from her straight path.

And as the trees disappeared and in their place was that abandoned barn in the backyard of Petra's home, a growl shook the earth, so menacing Grey swore it could've put the chill of winter back in the air. So she pushed on, not even realizing she was crying until she was banging on the back door with all her might. She didn't realize she was sobbing until the door swung open and she was looking a frightened Dimitri in the eyes.

"Grey?"

That was when the girl broke. She fell into his arms and let the sobs rip through her as he called for his grandmother and for Petra. She sobbed for herself, for putting herself in this situation and for Maksim who she left behind without a single glance. She sobbed for running from the beast, and she sobbed for staying this long. She sobbed at the thought of home, away from Russian soil, but mostly for the man she was falling for, the man who was cursed with a beast inside him that she feared with every fiber of her being.

"Poluchit' yeye vnutri!" The rough voice of Klara filled the air. "Do prikho-da khishchnik!"

In a swift motion, Grey was lifted into the air by Dimitri who was hushing her softly, whispering that everything was fine. She shivered at his touch that seemed cold and bland, nothing like his.

"Maksim. You have to go back for Maksim!" Grey was begging Dimitri as she was placed on the couch, just then remembering the eldest brother she found on the ground. Petra was rushing around locking doors and closing windows while Klara watched from behind Dimitri with tired eyes.

"Grey, calm down-"

"No!" Grey shoved Dimitri away as she continued to sob. "Please, you can't leave Maksim out there, he'll die!"

"Hush, girl." Klara stepped forward and used her free hand to cup Grey's cheek, the girl naturally leaning into her warm hand. "Oldest Volkov is strong. He survive."

"What if he doesn't?" Grey's voice broke and pity filled everyone's eyes.

"You still will."

Grey was silent for a moment, eyes taking in everyone before lingering on Petra who was crying. All of them were dressed in pajamas and their hair all messes, Grey realized it was the middle of the night and she filled with guilt as she turned back to Petra. She gave a sad smile towards her blonde haired friend before holding out her arms. Petra ran to Grey, wrapping their arms around one another as they both cried.

Petra kept repeating apologies over and over but Grey kept quieting her. "It's the past, Petra. Everything's fine."

Then Petra shot back, hands grabbing Grey's face. "Did he hurt you? I will kill him if he even tried to touch you, Grey, I-"

"I'm fine - I promise." Grey smiled at Petra before turning her eyes to Klara. "He's going to come for me before sunrise. When he does, I want you all locked somewhere safe -"

"Grey-"

"-I don't want anyone else getting hurt because of me."

"He knows not touch my family." Klara just about growled out. "After Ethen, I show him who is real beast here. He not kill another of my kin."

"And I won't let him touch you, Grey." Petra was filled with determination. "He won't get near you."

"No. You will all stay away if-I mean when he comes for me." The way Grey spoke made it hard to go against her. "You will not fight for me. You will let him take me."

"But Grey-"

"You will not put yourself in harms way for me. Understood?"

"As you wish."

~•~

TRANSLATIONS:"Poluchit' yeye vnutri!"Get her inside!

"Do prikhoda khishchnik!"Before the arrival of the predator!

Part Twenty Three

There were paintings that used to hang in the hall that was now barren; multiple beautiful paintings that Alexei had always loved to admire as a little boy, his favorite the one beside the room that held his mother's piano. His favorite painting was one of the darker ones that decorated the hall, it told such a strong, emotional story that the young boy couldn't understand on his own. He used to lean his head on his mother's shoulder as she perched him on her hip, telling him the story behind each and every one of her paintings.

She'd get to his favorite and she'd stop and stare at it in silence for awhile, her eyes holding a glint that he never got the chance to decipher. It was her favorite as well, for it held a memory that defined who that woman was. In the painting was a woman, her face hidden by her black cloak but her long black hair curled into visibility, falling down past her hips. Behind her back, gripped in thin fingers was a dagger that young Alexei had yet to see, with her other hand, she was grabbing brightly colored flowers from a little girl with bright red hair and dark eyes. The little girl wore dark colors yet her cherry red lips were pulled back in a white smile.

Alexei's mother would tell him the name, something in Italian that he never remembered, and tell him about that little girl. How the woman in the story met the girl and what their interaction entailed of. She'd tell him that the little girl disappeared after she gave the woman flowers, never to be seen again. His mother never told him honestly but now, thinking back on that painting, that was the first person his mother ever killed; that innocent little girl who only wanted to give her flowers. It was the beginning of an era of terror, the beginning of his mother's trail of blood, that only grew bigger and longer as her years went on.

That painting, and every single one of his mother's paintings now hung in the library where Maksim spent most of his time. Alexei occasionally visited only to admire his mother's work, and reflect on how he was like her - a murderer who regretted every kill. Every single one of those paintings held her victims in their last moments before she ended their lives, every detail of their bodies and faces etched into those canvases. A story of bloodshed and regret.

When the beast finally retreated to the back of Alexei's mind and let his human side reign, he stared at his brother who lay on the ground, eyes open now just staring at the sky; that regret his mother painted about flowed through his veins.

"Maksim."

"I'm fine. Grey-" He began to cough and Alexei sat him up, watching the blood leak from his lips.

"She's with Klara." The younger brother answered, guilt filling his veins. "She's safe now."

"She's not safe until she's with you."

• • •

Grey was shivering despite the blanket wrapped around her shoulders. Winter may be gone, but the early morning fog brought chills to Grey's pale skin that even the thickest blanket couldn't shield her from. She'd been inside the cabin with the silent family until the sun showed it's first signs in the dark night and only then did she move to sit on their stairs that lead to the backyard, looking out at the ominous trees.

The sun had risen quite a bit, the sky a gorgeous flaming orange to highlight the world at peace, tints of a daunting red highlighted the sky. There were birds chirping softly, little creatures crawling low in the dewy grass, the light morning fog creeping out of the tall trees. The world was alive with springtime.

Grey shivered again and out of nowhere, there he was, walking out of the trees in all of his dark and beautifully corrupted glory. She saw, for the first time, all the scars that littered his skin in the morning light, some old and faded and some bright pink as if they just scarred. She saw how with each step he took, his long legs carried him gracefully over the wet grass, muscles in every part of his body flexing with each movement. She saw his eyes as if she was seeing them for the first time again, that bright blue that seemed to shine like a flame when his eyes were upon her, the dark bags underneath them only seemed to highlight the blue. And she saw for the first time, a man with no beast. She saw Alexei Volkov, a man who had lost himself to the curse that plagued him but had still managed to find her in all the chaos. He had come back for her and she knew had she left last night, he still would've found his way to her. Because nothing could stop the beast from claiming what was his. And nothing in this world could stop a man from reaching his woman.

As he walked closer, Grey stood and she too began to move barefooted through the dewy grass. It was cold on her feet so she wrapped the blanket tighter around her as goosebumps rose across her skin. Whether the goosebumps rose from the chills or the way her body lit up under Alexei's fiery gaze, Grey wasn't too sure, probably both, but more so the latter. Upon reaching her, he placed a cold hand on her cheek and the other on the crook of her neck, right over his mark. His eyes scanned her up and down, checking for any injury and when he didn't find a single one, his lips were on hers.

The kiss was rough, it seemed that was all he knew, yet the passion pushed through his lips. It pushed through the way his lips moved against hers, and in the way he held onto her as if she'd run away at any second. So much passion behind his kiss that it left Grey stunned for a minute before she returned the kiss. And after a few moments in their own world, he pulled away to admire Grey's closed eyes and breathless, flushed look before the gray storm clashed with his eyes.

"I'm sorry."

Grey almost broke down again. "You have nothing to apologize for."

"I have everything to apologize for. There is nothing I can do or give you in this life that would amount for the sins I have committed just last night."

Grey didn't know what to say. There were no words in this world that could express what she felt. She wanted to tell him that he did nothing wrong, that everything was fine but deep down she knew that he did everything wrong and that she was terrified. But she'd never tell him that. So she simply shook her head and pulled a warm hand out from beneath her blanket to rest her hand over his cold one that lay on her cheek and she closed her eyes.

The way Alexei watched her was like no other. He took in every single detail on her face as her eyes shut and she took in a deep breath. From the three dark freckles spread around her right cheek, to the long brown eyelashes that hid those eyes of hers. He was bewitched by this girl; just him completely, for his beast had subsided to the dark corners of his mind and he felt purely human for a moment. And it seemed in that moment of humanity, he felt true feelings for the human girl before him and it rendered him breathless. It was the first time the beast was not pushing for control while around her and it let him see how much he had grown fond of the girl. These strange feelings were purely him. He wanted her just as bad as the beast inside of him did.

"Come home with me." He spoke soft, as if she would coil away from his words. "Come be my queen."

"Alexei-"

"I regret all that I have put you through. All the taunting and fear." He was so sincere Grey felt it in her chest. "Grey, you are the only food of mine I have wanted to keep around." Her light laugh was heaven to him. "Stay with me."

"What about my job? My friends?"

"They are nothing compared to the love that we could have."

"But truly, what about you?" Grey stepped back, sadness in her eyes. "Am I going to have to run from you, risk my life and watch you almost murder your brother every full moon until I learn to love that beast? I want to love you Alexei, I truly do but I fear the beast more than I've ever feared anything."

Alexei felt lost. He'd never had a person's words effect him in such a way that left him breathless, stumbling for words that seemed to lodge themselves in his throat. He knew at that moment he had fallen so incredibly hard and all he needed was for her to fall back, to get rid of the beast that kept her away from him.

"Forget about the beast, my lioness." Alexei begged, grabbing her hands beneath the blanket. "Focus on me and only me. Wish him away and he shall disappear and the world will be only ours. No beast. No fear. Nothing but love."

Grey was watching him, an emotion shimmering in those eyes of hers that he'd never seen before. They darted across his face and down to his hands that gripped hers, and when her eyes met his again, he could see all her emotions swirling in those stormy eyes. She was silent for a few tense moments before she finally opened her mouth to speak, but her voice never filled the air.

"That's a load of bullshit."

Part Twenty Four

{ translations in the comments!also i was totally gonna upload the prologue to Atlas but wattpad wanted to be a hoe and delete my prologue so now i have to rewrite it but it kinda works out because i've been wanting to make the people a little more "savage" or throw it back in time a little bit so ya girls about to do some MAJOR editing it's lit!!M xx}

He watched Grey whirl around and the eyes of the beast land on him. Her eyes were wide with confusion as she pressed her back against Alexei, her hand seeking his behind her. His eyes glared down at their interlocked fingers, ignoring the burning gaze from the beast.

"Dimitri, what are you doing out here?" Grey spoke soft as the beast behind her only growled and glared. He did not like another male getting close to what was his, let alone stand there like he was challenging him.

"Saving you that's what I'm doing, Grey." He spoke strong, voice full of confidence and lacking fear. "If you leave with him you will die."

Grey was growing angry fast. "What? Dimitri what is this about?"

"Back off, pup." The growl shook the beast's chest making Grey shiver against him. "Know your place."

"My place beneath you? Me acting as if you were my Alpha?" He laughed a dark laugh. "Fuck you, mate. That so-called 'place' was destroyed the minute you killed my love, my bonded." Dimitri was vicious, he had no ounce of kindness left in his body, eyes black pools of resentment towards Alexei.

"Sledit' za svoim yazykom mal'chik," Alexei's words were like poison on the tip of a serpent's sinister tongue. "Ili ya uberi eto."

"Da khishchnik, dalit' moy yazyk pered devushkoy, kotoruyu utverzh-dayut, chto lyubyat. Pokazat' yey, chto vy na a zver'. Pokazat' yey, grekhi chto proklyatiye ne mozhet skryt'. Dat' yey povod dlya zapuska."

Alexei was quick to move Grey behind him, a growl so vicious leaving his lips that it just about shook the whole ground. The world around them seemed to stop at the sound of his warning, everything grew silent. Grey didn't dare loosen her grip on his hand, she knew it was one of the only things holding him back and she wasn't about to let him hurt Dimitri in any way.

"Alexei." She murmured under the sharp gaze of Dimitri. "Just turn away. Don't let it take over, please. Breathe, my beast."

And just like that, Alexei's attention was focused solely on the girl who was staring at him as he turned to face her. He was fully ready to take the girl home and to places beyond. Nothing - no one - could separate them as long as he had a say, especially not this little boy who lived in the past. Grabbing Grey by both her hands, her pulled them up to place a kiss upon each hand. He'd grown so fond of the human girl, it was probably unhealthy for someone to feel so strongly towards another. She was his weakness, and while he accepted it, fate would have it that no one as hated as a beast like him, would have a weakness that wouldn't end in his ruin.

Her eyes were only on him. On those beautiful eyes of his that never failed to take her breath away and mesmerize her. He was her only focus, her only care in the world. Maybe if she hadn't been so entranced, maybe if she hadn't asked him to turn away, maybe if she had just gone home like he'd asked, everything could've been avoided.

The way all the breath in his lungs left him to fan across her hand that he had just placed a kiss upon. The way his eyes grew wide and the blazing blue seemed to dull and the flame in them fade away and in its place were bland ashes. The way crimson blood trickled from his mouth and left a trail from those full lips of his, all the way down his chin to drip down his neck. The way his body in front of her tensed and yet his grip on her hands lost it's strength. The way he lost his strength. His life.

Grey was petrified, her world was spinning in a downward spiral and everything was ringing so loud she couldn't even hear her own blood curdling scream as Dimitri yanked the silver dagger out of Alexei's back.

He fell out of her reach and down to the cold ground only for Grey to crumble with him and grab his face. She was crying so hard she shook while trying to make his unfocused eyes focus on her and only her but they wouldn't, they just stared at the sky as he shook and his body grew colder than the snow that once covered this land completely. Blood dribbled from his lips and the hole in his back to seep into the grass beneath them.

Finally Grey found her voice, her teary eyes glaring at Dimitri, screaming at him as Petra and her grandmother ran outside. "What have you done?!" She cried as the wind around them seemed to pick up.

"I did the world a favor!" Dimitri was offended that Grey was even crying, for in his mind he saved her, he saved her from a fate full of darkness and death. "You should be thanking me! I saved you!"

"Saved me? Saved me?! Dimitri I was happy! The only saving that needs to be done is Alexei!"

"You would've ended up dead, Grey, had I not killed the monster." He spat to the ground and Grey grew furious.

Standing to her feet she shoved Dimitri by the chest and moved so she was face to face with him. Gone was the girl sobbing for the life of her love and in her place was a girl so calm yet fire blazed in her eyes as she swore revenge. "If he doesn't come back, I swear to you that I will kill you. I will make you suffer. I will make you wish you were dead, Dimitri. You have my word!"

"You are making a mistake!-" Petra moved in and shoved Dimitri back, acting as a barrier between him and the rest of them as Klara found her way to Alexei.

Klara was knelt on one side of him as Grey reluctantly moved away from Dimitri and took to the other side. The old woman was already moving quick to steal her beast from her arms and turn him over, making sure to turn his head to the side, blank eyes looking towards Grey who was holding his limp hand in a bone crushing grip. She placed her wrinkled hands over the gushing wound and frowned.

"The silver is in his heart."

Grey grew panicked. "You can fix it though. . . Right, Klara? Please tell me you can save him."

"I can but I must warn you, bringing someone back to the land of the living, they are different." Grey frowned and the woman continued. "They lose apart of themselves when they die and return, he will not be the same as he was a moment ago."

"I don't care, Klara, just bring him back to me."

"Grey, listen-"

"I'm begging you to bring him back to me, Klara."

The old woman paused, her solemn eyes taking in the broken girl and she sighed. "As you wish."

• • •

Maksim had felt it from miles away, tucked in his room in their home. The feeling was so raw, so powerful that it had him stumbling and weak. It was a burning fire that rippled out from where his heart was placed, spreading across his chest and leaving a trail of pain down his spine. It was a feeling so real that he had to look down at his own chest and make sure there wasn't actually a knife in his heart. And when there was no blood, no knife, no more pain, he knew what had happened when the cold feeling of emptiness filled his veins. He felt his brother die. And for those few minutes that Maksim sat on the floor of his room, breathless and broken, he wondered what he was supposed to do in a life without his little brother. And sitting there, he had flashes of himself drinking himself to death in the home he grew up in. All alone. The vivid images of his baby brother's lifeless eyes, blood pooling around him, was enough to almost drive him off the edge. Memories, the good and the bad, so clear that Maksim thought he was reliving them, flashed behind his eyelids that he had squeezed shut. For a long few minutes, Maksim felt like his life was falling apart, piece by peace and he didn't know what to do.

And then, all of the sudden, the feeling lifted, and Maksim felt whole and normal again despite the confusion that raged in the back of his mind like a thunderstorm. He'd felt Alexei die, he remembered the feeling from his parents and it didn't disappear so quickly; it had slammed into him and settled in the deepest pits of his chest like heavy weights. Something had happened. Alexei was alive. So after the confusion had lifted, he managed to move himself from his dark room to the living room where he poured himself a glass of vodka and sat beside the window looking towards the forest, watching with dead, dull eyes, waiting.

And when they emerged from the forest, Alexei dominated the clearing, Maksim's eyes automatically going to him. The bags under his eyes and blood staining the skin around his lips and arms, droplets on his naked torso. He looked different, something about him seemed more feral, more beastly. But it wasn't even the bloodied beast he'd come to know as his brother that had him scared, it was the girl in his arms. An arm hooked under her knees and another behind her back, she lay limply across him. One of her pale arms was swinging by her side indicated the fact that she was unconscious, as well as her head that lay back at an awkward angle. She too was covered in blood. Maksim gulped.

He was quick to move out of the way for his brother who brushed past him and inside without a single glance. His cold eyes were set to nowhere in specific with a hard glares. Maksim was hot on his trail as he followed him into the living room where he dumped - quite literally - the unconscious Grey, who groaned when her body collided with the sofa in a bounce; she thankfully didn't bounce onto the ground.

"What the hell, brother?" Maksim was infuriated. From his brother's death scare to this and he had not one answer, he was pissed. And it seemed all that anger inflated when he caught sight of the marks from Grey's shoulder and across her collarbone, ending just above her chest and directly above her beating heart. The wounds oozed blood onto her shirt and the couch and Maksim was by the human girl's side in an instant.

"What have you done?!" He yelled after a silent moment of inspecting her with his little brother standing to the side not even looking at the girl.

Alexei shrugged. "She got in the way."

And with that, Alexei walked out of the room and disappeared up the stairs.

ATLAS

I JUST PUBLISHED THE PROLOGUE TO MY NEW BOOK GO CHECK IT OUT OMMMGGG

LOTS OF LOVE!!

M XX

Part Twenty Five

Maksim stood in shock for a few solid moments, staring at the space where his little brother once was. Or should he say, the imposter in his little brother's body. He hadn't seen such eyes devoid of emotion since his father. Even when Alexei had his moments of more murderous beast than human, when he'd come home covered in the blood of innocents, there was still a spark of remorse in his eyes, guilt for what he'd done but just then, Maksim had seen nothing.

Snapping out of his trance, he was quick to grab a towel and a bowl filled with cold water before returning to Grey. She was still out cold, her eyes twitched and moved beneath her lids, her skin pale and balmy. His eyes found the claw marks that started from her right collar bone and ripped through her skin all the way to just above her heart. Maksim had to bite back his anger. He sucked in a deep breath and released it slowly before dipping the little towel in the bowl and beginning to clean away the blood on Grey's wound.

After just a few moments, the bowl held water stained pink, no longer pure and clean. Grey's breathing had become sharp intakes every time he touched her wound and he could see her brows furrow in pain, yet she never woke. Maksim had begun to hum a soft melody because the silence that had blanketed itself across the house didn't settle well with him, it was eerie and almost sinister.

He couldn't figure it out, why his brother would do this, especially to the girl he bonded. The look in his eyes when he brought Grey was something Maksim thought he'd never see in Alexei again, something he hadn't seen since they were young.

He could still remember their first days living alone, just the two of them as Maksim mourned and Alexei raged. He'd leave in the evening and wouldn't return until early morning, by then he'd be covered in the blood of innocent humans and despite his monstrous exterior, the look in his eyes would say it all. Guilt, remorse, self-hatred, so many emotions would wrap into one big wave in his eyes and some nights he'd sob to Maksim, on the worst nights, he'd stare at the wall and, despite his young age, drink himself close to death. Maksim was always there to bring him back for a short period of time.

"Maks?"

Grey. Her eyes were staring up at him, shining with unshed tears and swirling with fear as she held the wrist of the hand that was dabbing at her wound, her grip loose and weak. She was shaking like a leaf.

"It's okay, Grey-"

"He's not himself, Maks." Her voice was just a whisper as the tears started to stream down her cheeks. "Klara, she did something when she brought him back and now-" She choked on her words.

The strength in her hand seemed to return and she was gripping his wrist so tight her nails dug into his skin. He opened his mouth to speak but the words that left Grey's mouth struck fear even in Maksim's blood.

"The beast is in control."

• • •

Alexei could hear her crying downstairs and his thoughts weren't of pity or sympathy but annoyance. He could hear his brother comforting her, his voice soft and it irritated him. Why would his brother put up with such a weak girl? And goddamn, why did she cry so much?

There was a part of him, deep down inside, that itched with the urge to go and hold her and protect her but the overpowering emptiness flowed in his veins. This feeling confused him. He hadn't felt so numb since his mother died, since he was more beast than man and when his only thoughts consisted of killing and blood. He knew something was wrong, but he didn't know why, what. Any time it seemed he'd break through the wall in his mind, he'd get shoved back and the beast would creep forward more.

He began to think, trying to remember why the girl called Grey seemed so fond of him. Why she would've cried over him and why she was there when he woke up on the ground before he beheaded the boy who stuck the dagger in his back.

Mine

The word echoed in his head, growled out by a vicious voice that hardly sounded human. Yet in that voice, in the body of the beast, was an over-whelming feeling of pain, of sadness that he didn't know the beast was capable of. What had happened to break the unbreakable beast?

And then that sadness was gone, replaced by that lust for blood and the urge to let the beast be free again. So Alexei unleashed his beast, not knowing what chaos would soon ensue.

• • •

It was the time of night between late and early when Grey awoke. The sky was dark and the world was silent - peaceful almost. The wounds on her body were burning with each intake of breath and when she tried to move it only intensified. So she gave up, laying there and praying for sleep but there was a feeling that wrapped itself around her body and chilled her veins that made her unable to sleep. Finally, when the feeling didn't leave, she pushed through the pain and sat up sharply. All the breath was knocked from her lungs and pain shot through her body. She sat for a few solid minutes before pushing herself to stand and walking out of the room all the while clutching her chest.

Using the wall as her leverage, Grey managed to make it downstairs and was on her way to the kitchen when the front door slammed open and she shrieked. She spun around so fast her wounds opened up again and she was left breathless, once again, at the pain and at the sight of him.

He stood there, in the doorway, chest heaving up and down, glowing eyes locked on an unmoving Grey. Standing bare and naked, Grey was able to see all the blood that stained his body. It was everywhere.

She hurried over to him as he shut the door and tried to move up the stairs. "Are you hurt?" He growled. "Don't growl at me I'm trying to help!"

"I don't need your help." His voice was deep, shockingly so.

"You've got blood all over you!"

He stared at her with his flaming eyes and teeth bared. "It's not mine."

With that he pushed her to the ground and stomped up the stairs as Maksim came rushing down. Neither brother even spared the other a single glance, one too focused on his bloodlust and the other focused on a teary-eyed Grey.

Her voice was soft as she asked Maksim, "What did I do?"

"None of this is your fault, Grey." He helped her stand. "Don't feel guilty."

"Who did he kill?" Her eyes were now wide with fear. "Oh Maks, you've got to go figure it out! What if-"

"Grey." He spoke and sat her down on the couch, crouching to eye level with her. "There's nothing we can do-"

"How did you get him back after it happened before?" She was begging him. "I want Alexei, back. I don't want the beast, I want him."

Maksim emphasized every word he spoke. "There is nothing we can do. You need to worry about yourself right now, you're weak and one wrong move can have you fighting for your life."

"But Maks-"

"Grey."

She was fighting back tears as he went to go get more gauze to wrap Grey's chest with. And after cleaning it up and rewrapping her, he sent her back to bed and made sure her door was locked before he himself ventured into the trees to right his brother's wrong.

Just like old times.

~•~

By the time Maksim reached the town, it was just before sunrise. Thankfully no one was out as he prowled through the town as a large wolf, following the foul stench of death. Everything was silent as he walked quietly, so silent it worried him.

Then, all of a sudden, there they were.

Down a road that led south of the town, a road that held less houses and more trees either side of it than the others. On this road Maksim found bodies among bodies trailing down it. Bloody paw-prints lead to his brother, the humans would blame it on an animal attack but he knew Petra and the witch would be wary.

As he walked along the road, he had to force himself not to look away, not to turn back, for the sight was one even Maksim couldn't handle. His brother was dirtier than he'd been before, his kills were normally clean, while this one, each and every single person, all 25 of them - Maksim had counted - were torn limb from limb, heads ripped off and guts laying in the open.

He wanted to throw up.

And as the sun began to rise, he could see their faces, their lifeless eyes all staring up at the colorful sky, and he felt everything his brother should've. And he wept.

And when the voices began to approach, it took everything in him to pull himself away from the open and to hide in the shadows. He couldn't force himself to leave them until he knew they were taken care of properly. But he regretted staying the minute they were found by a man, who immediately got the whole town. He regretted staying to watch when he saw the families approach slowly. They stumbled forward, some stood back with wide eyes, too shocked to move, but everyone as they reached their person wept. They wept and they screamed. They yelled to the heavens, begging for their person back, pleading, asking why, why them?

Then there, in the back of the crowd stood Petra, watching it all with cold eyes. Maksim could see it in her eyes. She knew. And somehow he knew that everyone in the town would soon know too.

••••

it's short but the end is approaching *cries because i don't want it to end yet* ~M xx

Part Twenty Six

When Grey awoke in her room, everything was silent, eerily so. So silent that the creaking of her bed as she sat up seemed impossibly loud. She was confused, still half asleep and drowsy but confused nonetheless as she tried her hardest to hear even the slightest sound in the house, but there was nothing. With careful movements and quiet steps, Grey made her way downstairs to find what she expected: a completely empty home. No breakfast waiting for her, no empty vodka glasses, everything was untouched and felt abandoned.

Grey sat in the kitchen for awhile, waiting for anything to happen but when nothing did she returned upstairs for a shower. After a long shower and dressing, she grabbed her camera, tied up her wet hair and made her way out of the silent house. She stopped outside for a minute, staring at the trees as if the brothers she'd grown so fond of would walk out of them at any moment but there wasn't even a rustle of leaves coming from the forest. It seemed as if time had stopped in the world, and everything was still and silent except for Grey. This made an uneasy feeling stir in the pit of her stomach. Something wasn't right.

As she looked around at the land that surrounded this old abandoned castle-like mansion, she found familiarity warming her veins and that feeling of being home - a feeling she hadn't felt since her mother died. Closing her eyes, she breathed in the scent of a nature so deep so it could embed itself in her lungs and sprout life inside of her. Life that she so desperately needed. She then tilted her head back so her eyes opened to the sky, looking up in search of any sign of God looking out for her but as it seemed lately, he was nowhere to be found. With a sigh from somewhere deep in her lungs, she trekked into the trees that everyone called enchanted, but she preferred the term "possessed" when describing the demon trees.

Deeper and deeper she traveled, stopping occasionally to bring her camera to her face to snap a few pictures of the environment. The silence in the air had slowly turned less int an eerie silence, and more of a peaceful one with the sounds of little wildlife around her. In the distance the sound of soft running water calmed her wild nerves, so she followed it until she reached a small stream running back in the direction of the old castle she'd grown so used to. Snapping a few quick pictures, she sat down beside the stream and just watched the water flow. For some reason it calmed her, it cleared her head enough so she could think of the situation rationally.

Yet if she hadn't been lost in her thoughts, Grey might've heard the creaking of the trees around her as the dark magic moved their roots.

Then, he was coming. She heard him before she saw him and she knew he had known where she was long before she was aware of his approaching presence. Grey didn't even bother turning her head in his direction despite the low growling that rumbled against his teeth. She just closed her eyes and leaned her head back to the sky as he continued to growl behind her.

"If you're just going to stand there and snarl at me then leave please." Grey snapped, her head turning to face the wolf with blazing eyes. "You're ruining my peace."

His growls got louder against his bared teeth and he took a step closer.

"I said leave me alone, Alexei!"

He snapped at her and Grey grew furious, her nostrils flaring, body rigid from both anger and fear. Grey was ready to burst at him, to yell and scream until he left but when she opened her mouth nothing came out from her lips. She gave a sigh and ran her hands down her face after she turned away from Alexei and back to the stream.

"You've ruined me Alexei Volkov." Her voice was but a whisper but the wolf heard it and the growling stopped. "You ruined me so beautifully and I hate it."

There was a long silence and when Grey turned around, she found that she was alone yet again. She sighed, biting back the tears that so desperately wanted to fall, and looked at the flowing water to distract herself. Her thoughts wanted to go to Alexei, she wanted to find him, she wanted to talk to him but she knew she couldn't. She couldn't do that when he was like this; a beast.

She pushed herself up despite the pain in her chest and turned back to the trees, but her heart dropped.

They'd moved.

"Are you kidding me?!" She groaned.

Grey scanned the area, her bottom lip tucked between her teeth as she tried to find trees that looked familiar. She found nothing. They wanted her to go somewhere, that much she knew but she didn't want to let them lead her, but for some reason, this feeling pushed her into the trees and let them guide her. It was the feeling in the pit of her belly that pushed her to walk into the trees, something that was telling her she needed to listen to them. Something deep within her was screaming at her to run to wherever they were leading her, yelling at her to hurry but she was wary. The trees had a way of screwing her over and she didn't want to know how they planned on doing it now. Yet, she followed them and watched them move to form a path for her.

And then, the trees thinned out and in their place was the town she'd stayed in; Petra's town. Her heart ached for that family and she had the urge to just see them, to just go hug them, to apologize for all that's happened; but the tug in her body pulled her in the opposite direction of her home.

Walking through the town streets was odd, not only because she hadn't been here in so long, but because there was not a single soul in the streets or outside. It was oddly silent despite this low murmur from the direction she was following. The farther she walked, the louder the murmur got and the more she realized it wasn't a murmur, it was angry voices and vicious sobs. Her stomach turned and her throat closed. The pull in her belly turned heavy and she suddenly found it harder to walk closer.

Grey stuck to the shadows when she got closer, close enough to make out all the villagers faces and the voice of the one standing in the middle of a murder scene.

Petra stood among bodies, her face contorted in anger as she spoke violent words in her native tongue. Grey couldn't pick up a single word, but whatever she was spitting was creating a flame inside the villagers as they yelled along with her. Some were throwing their fists in the air as she screamed, the passion in her tone overwhelming.

"We cannot sit idly by any longer! Our people are getting slaughtered and we are doing nothing! It is not a simple animal that has done this. No! It is a beast! A beast that can lure men and women and children from the safety of their homes and drag them to their death. And yet, this is no average beast. . . This is a beast - a wolf that walks among us in a sheeps skin! He walks among us as a human! I've seen it with my own eyes, I've watch a human man transform into a wolf before my own eyes. He is real and he is a murdered. He murdered my brothers and he has murdered our loved ones!

This beast must be killed! We can destroy him with our numbers, with our vengeance! He deserves something far worse than the serenity that death would grant him, but the best we can do is slaughter him like he has done to our own. . . If you help me, I can lead you to him. He and his brother live in our forest, right in our backyard - two beasts right under our noses! I can take you to them and we can end this reign of suffering. Help me, I beg of you, avenge my brothers and your wives, your sisters and brothers, your fathers and families! Help me kill the beast!"

"Kill the beast!"

They were yelling, screaming and crying. Petra looked upon the chaos with a smile and tears of her own, while Grey looked upon it all with shock. She watched as Petra turned to her grandmother and whisper English words that she'd never forget.

"We end the Volkov reign tonight."

Grey stumbled back from the crowd, tripping over her own feet and falling to the ground. She was panicking, breathing too heavy and too fast, trying to move too quickly while her mind couldn't catch up - it was stuck on the image of Petra killing Alexei and Maksim. She wanted to cry, scream and kill Petra all at once - but she was leaning more towards breaking down and crying. Yet she still managed to pull herself together for another second and push herself to the trees where she broke into a sprint.

Weaving in and out of the tall trees, running in the direction of the castle-like house she'd learned to love, Grey felt tears streaming down her face as images of the townspeople tearing apart the brothers. Images of their lifeless eyes flashed across her mind and brought more tears to her eyes, and when her eyesight started to blur with tears, she let the trees lead her in the right direction.

And when she broke through the trees, the house in view, Grey was screaming their names. She needed one of them, beast or not, she needed one of them to know. She needed to save them.

Part Twenty Seven

Maksim heard her screaming from a mile away. He'd been deep in the trees, in a area where he always found himself when he was troubled: sat in front of the tree they buried their mother under. He was in the middle of talking to her spirit softly when he heard Grey's voice screaming his name and his brother's name, the raw emotion in her pleas made his heart stop. He wasted no time in sprinting through the trees himself to meet Grey in the clearing around the house and when she saw him she burst into a heavy fit of tears and collapsed.

"Grey?!" He ran faster than ever to reach her and he fell to her side and tried to lift her up. "Grey, what's going on? What happened?"

She was clutching to him, her hands shaking violently. She was stuttering out her words, tripping over them and choking on them, her fear getting the best of her tongue.

"Grey." Maksim grabbed her face in his hands and made her eyes meet his steady gaze. "Look at me. Breathe. Calm down and breathe. What's happened?"

"Petra." Her voice was so soft and broken it broke Maksim's own heart. "She-She got the people in the town-they. ." She started shaking her head back and forth with tears running down her face.

He hushed her, pulling her into a tight hug as she sobbed into his chest. "Maks, they're gonna come. They're gonna kill you."

Maksim tensed, his whole being screamed at him to go to the town and kill them before they could even touch him or his brother, but the crying girl in his arms gave him his humanity. He needed to find his brother, to kill those bastards that wanted to harm them, to protect his family and the girl in his arms, but in order to do that, he need to get Grey to safety first. His first priority was her.

So he scooped her up in his arms, despite her protests and questions, he stayed silent and hurried back to his home. Maksim's mind was racing, this wasn't the first time they'd been hunted down by humans and he knew it wouldn't be the last, but this time there was so much more on the line - the life of yet another person, but this life was more precious than him and his brother's combined. He promised himself and the heavens above that if Alexei couldn't do it, he'd protect Grey with his life.

Grey had calmed down by the time he walked inside his home, but the minute she noticed the presence of another in the same room as them, she was shaking again.

"Brother."

Alexei growled at Maksim, though he lacked humanity, he didn't like another male touching what was his. Grey noticed his and crawled out of Maksim's arms but her hands were wrapped around his bicep, the only thing keeping her from collapsing. Alexei stepped forward and Maksim returned the growl.

"Don't come near her." Maks was tense as he stared into soulless eyes.

Alexei tilted his head to the side and watched the pair like the predator he was. "You seem to have forgotten she is mine, brother, not yours."

"I have not. We have bigger problems though Alexei." He began to speak to his brother in their native tongue.

Grey watched on with curious eyes as their words rolled smoothly off their tongues, venomous words and bloody threats flowing with them. Both brothers looked murderous when her name slid off Maksim's tongue, the word sticking out among the foreign words. She dragged her eyes to Alexei, his whole demeanor screamed monster, his body tense and ready to kill. His eyes met hers.

His words came out in English. "They're fools if they think they can harm us. I'll have their heads at their feet before they can touch us."

And then he was gone and Maksim was turning Grey around to look into his eyes. "Listen to me closely. Inside my nightstand is a knife, get it and go lock yourself in Alexei's room. It's the only one with a lock. Do not come out for anyone unless me, do you understand me?"

"Maksim! I'm not going to lock myself away while you both get murdered!" Grey was shaking her head, tears stinging her eyes again. "Maybe-Maybe if I go to them they'll-"

"Grey. . . This is far deeper than my brother taking you. We have to pay for our sins eventually and I don't want you getting caught up in the flames. They will kill you if you defend us, they will not hesitate. You still have a chance at life, you and Alexei can make it. I will fight for you."

"Maks-"

"Go. They're close."

"Maksim!"

"Go, Grey! Now!"

He gave her a violent push towards the stairs before running out of the front door, leaving Grey stunned and frozen at the bottom of the stairs. She was torn. On one hand, she trusted them to be able to defend themselves, to be able to win, but on the other, something inside her was screaming at her to help them. With a sigh, she ran up the stairs to follow Maksim's directions.

~•~

Outside, hidden in the trees, Maksim found his brother once again, watching for any sign of movement with these predatory eyes. He was not being hunted - he was doing the hunting. The calmness that could be seen in his eyes though, it was unsettling. His bonded's life was at risk and he looked like he could care less, yet on the inside, his mind was raging with thoughts of protecting her and only her.

He was a beast but the beast would do anything for her.

"We should've been better prepared." Alexei broke the silence with a rumble of a growl. "We should've known they'd come again. We should've just killed them all the last time."

"Just because we are cursed to be beasts doesn't mean we have to act like it."

"It's in our blood. We were born to be monsters, to have blood on our hands." Alexei was staring forward, eyes still on watch. "You just have to accept it."

"If we don't have to kill them all-"

"They threatened my family. They will all die."

"Alexei-"

He held up his hand to silence his older brother. His body becoming tense and his muscles starting to coil beneath his skin - he was preparing for a battle.

"They're close." Maksim stated the obviously, his own other side bristling with anticipation. He began to strip, ready to shift.

"The girl?" Alexei asked quietly.

"She's safe." Was all Maksim needed to say before his brother gave a nod and he began to change into his wolf.

Alexei stayed as a human. The beast was already out, there was no point in the vulnerability that comes with the shift. He wouldn't risk it. He wouldn't give the humans the satisfaction of killing him even in the most cowardly ways.

Not now. Not ever.

They'd never kill him. He'd never let them even get close.

~•~

Grey was shaken up with the feeling of a weapon in her hands.

She'd never been one for violence, never saw the point in it. Violence solves nothing. So, naturally, she'd never really owned a weapon before, never held a knife other than a kitchen knife, never touched a gun. Yet the knife in her hands felt like it almost belonged there as oddly as it sounded. It was large and clunky, its blade not incredibly long but it was wide, it's point sharp and edges jagged, the handle was heavy in itself and Grey's slender fingers had a hard time wrapping around it.

But it felt like it was meant to be in her hands.

She had a weird feeling in her belly, like everything that was happening was supposed to happen. Like the knife was supposed to be in her hands, like she was supposed to be curled underneath the window of Alexei's room with her knees to her chest, like she was supposed to be locked in this damned home while the brothers were supposed to be outside fighting to protect themselves and her. This feeling unsettled her.

Even from inside, Grey was able to hear when they came. She heard the roar from the beast, from khishchnik, that beast in the legend was in those woods once again; no longer was he that boy she was supposed to save, he was a cold-blooded killer. She heard growls that she knew came from Maksim and she sent a silent prayer that he'd be okay. She could heard the war cries from the lips of the townspeople, the sounds of them being slain and them trying to slay the wolves. She heard all the sounds from the bloodbath outside that she was too engulfed to notice the sounds coming from the inside, like the sound of windows being broken and a door being kicked in.

She didn't hear them inside until it was a voice calling up from the front door.

"Grey?!"

She knew that voice. That fucking voice. Petra. Had she come in the beginning, Grey would've ran out of this room and into her awaiting arms. . . But now, Grey recoiled at the sound of her, fear and disgust making her heart race. Her grip on the knife tightened. She pressed up silently, her legs shaking from god knows what at this point, her eyes darted from the door to the window and she almost fell over at the sight.

Red.

So much red.

It seeped into the ground, covered trees and humans. It covered the bodies that lay scattered and leaked from their pores. Most of the townspeople lay in that crimson stained grass, their eyes looking into the heavens where their souls sat.

"Grey!"

Her voice was getting closer, too close for Grey's liking and she began to panic. She didn't know what to do, but she knew despite all the hate she harbored for Petra, she couldn't kill her. It wasn't in her nature. So she pushed herself into the corner where the open door would hide her and covered her mouth to make her breathing as silent as possible as Petra's footsteps crept down the hall.

"Grey. . . I know you're here." She sighed. "Don't do this. Don't defend them. I want to help you, save you."

Grey wanted to scoff.

The doorknob to the door she was in jiggled and she froze. Petra had found her and no doubt she could hear her racing heart.

"Open the door, Grey."

Silence.

"God dammit open it Grey!" The door shook under the force of her fist. "Don't me me do this! I don't want to hurt you!"

Grey couldn't bite back her words. "You hurt me when you arranged to kill my wolf and his brother."

"Grey! He doesn't love you! He can't love you he's a beast!" Petra pounded on the door again. "You're delusional! Let me help you before they kill you!"

"If you want to help me then leave!"

Silence.

Grey thought she'd left but her voice scared her, the softness yet deadliness in her tone made her tense.

"I didn't want to do this."

She broke down the door.

~•~

How did he allow himself to end up in this position? How did he end with his hands tied behind his back and his head yanked back with a knife to his throat?

Protecting his brother.

Beast or not, Alexei recognized blood - pack - and he risked his life to save Maksim's.

He'd found him in the clearing outside the house, fighting the few humans left so he didn't notice the one hiding in the trees with a gun. The bullet went straight into Alexei's leg and it began to burn, sting in a way he'd never experienced. Whatever they'd put in it was burning him from the inside out and he screamed. The noise distracted Maksim and the next thing they knew, they were both bound with ropes coated in whatever had been in the bullet, side-by-side with knives to their throats.

They didn't slice them across their skin though, they just held it there as they waited for something; and that something was Petra.

He'd begun to grow bored, irritated with the waiting and was trying to break out if the burning ropes but he felt weak, too weak to unleash his fury. He could see Maksim out of the corner of his eyes doing the same thing, wiggling his hands in a way to loosen the ropes. It wasn't working well.

Then, all of the sudden, she screamed.

He knew it was her and as much as he wanted to roll his eyes and focus on saving himself, there was that something inside of him that was panicking. Maksim was frozen, his eyes wide as they watched the front door.

"Alexei!"

He snapped his head to his brother who didn't look fazed. Alexei was in war mode, he was even more beast than man and he did not care whether Grey died, only himself and his brother. Maksim's head snapped back to the door just in time to see Grey being dragged out by her arms by two men. She was screaming, yelling, kicking and flailing her body around, trying to get out but nothing worked. He could see the tears fill her eyes when she saw him and his brother and it caused her to fight more.

"Alexei!"

His brother didn't even blink at her. He stared at her as if she was a stranger. It broke Maksim's heart.

Petra followed shortly behind them and she smirked at the sight of the brothers looking so vulnerable.

"Well, well, well boys." She clapped her hands together. "Isn't this a compromising situation." The smile on her face pissed them off and they both growled at her. "Like the ropes? Silver's a bitch."

"You're a bitch." Alexei grumbled and her head snapped to the side.

"Alexei Volkov. . ." He growled at her. "You're the reason all this is happening. You're the beast we want dead and it's your fault that your brother is being brought down with you. Everything that happens today is because of you."

"Petra stop this!" Grey yelled from behind her, still struggling in the men's grip. She had tears running down her cheek. "This isn't going to solve anything!"

Petra spun around and glared at Grey. "If you know what's best for you, you'd shut your mouth. I don't want to hurt you so don't try to defend them!"

Grey scoffed. "I won't let you hurt them. I won't."

"And what are you gonna do, huh? You're human! Just because you're bonded to a beast doesn't make you one. You're weak. You can't save them."

"Fuck you!" Grey spat at her, hot, angry tears pouring from her eyes more now. "You're the beast! Revenge won't bring your brothers back! It won't bring anyone back so just stop being a fucking cunt and let us go!"

Petra's hand connected with Grey's cheek with a loud crack.

Silence engulfed the forest around them, the only sound that could be heard was Grey's ragged breathing before a sinister growl rumbled the very earth below them.

"Do not touch her." The voice that came from Alexei's voice was not Alexei. It was pure, raw anger coming from the deepest and darkest pits of that beast inside him. Emotionless monster or not, someone harmed what was his. He wanted Petra's blood.

"Or what?!"

Everything happened so fast it was hard for even the most supernatural eyes to keep up.

One second, Alexei was kneeled and bound beside his brother and the next his claws were tearing into the men who held him back from the female wolf who threatened his family. Blood splattered all over him and on those around them as he tore their throats from their skin and their hearts from their chests.

It all happened so fast no one had time to prepare.

Yet there was Grey, watching it all in slow motion it seemed. Every muscle and tendon tore and ripped painfully slow in front of her.

So slow she could see the beast as he really was, what she should've been fearing this whole time instead of falling for.

So slow she saw the other alive men drag Maksim further from his brother as he too tried to fight against the ropes.

So slow she watched the men holding Maksim draw their knives and bury them in his skin.

So slow she watched the way his eyes widened and he froze.

So slow she saw Petra reach for the gun holstered on her hip.

And then it moved so fast she missed what happened next.

Because one second she blinked and everything was unfolding in front of her so slow, and the next she only saw blue.

A blue, beautiful clear sky.

Another blink and there was Alexei's face hovering over her, his eyes so wide and fearful - so human - it broke her heart. He was saying something to her but her ears were ringing and she couldn't hear him. She frowned as she reached a hand up to touch his face and froze when her hand was covered in blood.

Grey could feel herself start to hyperventilate as she slowly turned her shaky hand over and over, finding only her palm coated with that crimson liquid. And when she lifted her head to look down, it felt like the heaviest thing she'd ever touched but she managed to lift it with the help of a hand behind her head.

The first thing she saw was Maksim a few feet away; she couldn't hear him but by the way his mouth was open wide and his face was contorted with pain, she could tell he was screaming as he ripped knife after knife out of his skin. He was surrounded by dead bodies of the men who had just been holding him captive.

Then, there it was. A large, dark spot of that dammed blood staining the front of her shirt just below her chest. And everything came flooding back.

She remembered breaking from the hold of the men and running in front of Alexei just as Petra pulled the trigger. The bullet had lodged itself into her body yet she was able to watch as shock took over Petra's body and she dropped the gun and stumbled back. She remembered the silence that followed the gunshot. She remembered Petra repeating the word 'no' over and over again as she stumbled away from Grey. And she remembered the roar that left Alexei's throat as she fell to the ground.

She didn't remember what followed but she probably didn't want to know.

And now, everything hit her: her hearing, her feeling, her senses all came back at once and she gasped.

~•~

Just as fast as the bullet left the chamber and entered Grey's body, Alexei's humanity had snapped back on. It hit him like a freight train and he almost fell back - watching the girl his beast chose as his, choose his life over her own was his awakening. He had to gather his composure for a minute before what just happened really registered in his mind.

He lets out a roar as he almost rips the arms off of the men who are left alive, trying to grab at him to contain him. They're trying to hold him back from Grey, from his little lion. They're trying holding him back from her as she shudders and shivers with her eyes watching the sky.

He's growling, screaming and crying by the time he tears out the last his captors throat and Grey seems like she's miles away when he only runs a few feet to reach her.

Grey's sight began to grow blurry as she takes in the sight of Alexei; she can't tell if she's losing vision from her tears or if that's death creeping in on her. It didn't matter either way. The only thing that mattered was Alexei. The look in his eyes broke her. For there, holding her in his arms, was the little boy from that painting in the room she'd found the day he kissed her, his eyes so full of this childlike sadness she broke. He looked so lost as his eyes darted from her own to the wound below her chest, he didn't know what to do - how to save her and he hated it.

Everything that happens today is because of you. Petra's words echoed in his head and he sobbed.

To them two, there was no one watching them, no one threatening to kill them. They were in their own world.

"Don't leave me, my lioness." He pleaded with her, his own eyes welling with fat tears that rolled down his cheeks.

Grey couldn't think about anything other than how pretty his eyes looked when he cried.

"I beg of you, don't leave me like this. I'm so sorry. I'm sorry. I'm so sorry. Don't leave me, Grey."

His words echoed on repeat in her head, her hearing fading in and out with her vision. She fought back, blinking her eyes over and over again -

she couldn't lose sight of those eyes of his. Alexei was clear again but the edges of her vision were turning dark and she felt heavy all of the sudden, so heavy she could barely breathe.

"I'm sorry I didn't give you the love you deserved."

She shook her head at him and a ragged breath was released and another slow one sucked in. Alexei shook. "I've loved you since I took your picture."

And he broke.

And she grew limp.

And he broke a thousand times over again.

Everything that happens today is because of you.

Epilogue

Days turned into weeks, that turned into years. He sat in his own lonely castle, watching the leaves change as he drank bottle after bottle of liquor until his entire cellar was empty and he was left with nothing but his thoughts.

The front door stayed unlocked, as did every other door and window on the property. Because no matter what, he didn't fully believe his love wasn't returning. He wanted to believe she'd come running through that door with cheeks tainted pink from the harsh Russian air, with those eyes of her wide as they looked at him.

Those goddamn eyes; they haunted him.

Every hour spent awake was because every time he closed his eyes, he was haunted with memories of her and those beautiful eyes. The silent house never helped much, and now that the beast inside of him was absent, he had absolutely no one.

Yet each day, he'd make the hard walk through the forest to find one specific tree. For in a little clearing, a single tree stood tall and proud, its leaves never falling to the ground, and beneath that everlasting piece of natural art was her. Buried six feet under right beside their mother.

He still remembered the day he and his brother dug the hole and placed her in it. She looked peaceful. Maksim had placed flowers in her hair and all around her body, he'd said they weren't her favorite, simple, sweet white roses that matched the paleness of her dress, but it was all he could get. He himself didn't have the courage to say anything, but simply listened with tears threatening to spill as his brother said the most magnificent words; and that still didn't do her justice.

Grey Clarke was unlike any other and goddamn did she deserve more than this.

He missed her, every second of every day. She'd given him a blessing and curse, in loving him and ridding him of the lycan curse, but now that he was human and his brother was gone too, he'd become quite acquainted with the feelings of complete and utter loneliness. Isolation was not kind to him.

Maksim left for America two months after Grey left. He'd said he couldn't stand the silence anymore and found solace in a place in the Rocky Mountains, somewhere he could embrace isolation with his wolf spirit and no one else. He didn't call, he didn't write, Alexei didn't even know if he was still alive or not but he knew deep down he couldn't die so easily - he was a true-born lycan, he was a fighter. Alexei believed though, that Maksim had harbored more feelings than a protective big brother towards Grey, and her death impacted him just as much as it did himself. He saw the way he lost the spark in his eyes after just a week, he'd lost his will to live, his light had been put out. Maksim loved Grey with every fiber of his being and losing her was like losing a part of him.

Alexei wished he'd lost only a part of him.

His heart stopped beating when Grey's did and his soul got buried with her that day.

He regretted all the times he made her cry. All the times he made her angry and all the times he told himself he hated her, that he didn't want her. He regretted not loving her and embracing her the way she deserved, because now she was cold in the ground and he was alone and cold in his own sense. He regretted everything and he wished he could go back in time to just tell her to leave Russia and never come back. He wished he could've warned her. The only thing that had given Alexei peace after her death was when he tore Petra's head from her body. But that was too short lived to mask the emptiness he felt inside.

The sound of a phone ringing somewhere in the house scared Alexei at first, it was the most noise he'd heard since Grey. It took him a minute to register what it was and practically sprinted upstairs to the room Grey stayed in, her phone buzzing atop the dresser. He didn't even look at the screen as he answered it.

"Grey?"

He knew he was stupid for believing she'd be calling her own phone - she was dead for fucks sake, but there was this tiny bit of hope inside of him that pleaded to the heavens for it to be her, alive and okay.

"Alexei."

Maksim.

He sounded good. He sounded like he hadn't spent the last few years sulking and trying to drink himself to death. He sounded happy. Alexei wanted to cry.

"Brother." He breathed. "Why'd you call her phone?"

"I knew you'd answer." Maksim's voice was smooth and calm. He sounded like he'd finally found peace. "I was worried you wouldn't though. I thought you might've. . ."

He didn't need to say it, they both knew what he meant. "I don't have the courage brother. The one time I can actually die just by even the smallest things, I lack the courage to actually do it." Alexei ran a hand down his face and sank to the floor, his head resting against the wall. As he breathed in the stale, almost gone scent of Grey that lingered in this room. He almost broke again. "How are you?"

He hesitated. "Good, brother. I'm really good."

"I'm glad."

"You should come to America. I found a pack buried in the mountains, their Alpha has become a close friend of mine, they'd greet you with open arms."

Alexei was so silent for the longest time, Maksim had thought he'd hung up. He called his name and he finally answered. "I want to, Maks, I do. I just-I can't leave her. I know she's dead and I know she's not coming back but I keep praying that she will and I cannot leave until she returns to me."

"Alexei, I found her family before I came here-"

"What?!"

"-I had to tell them. I left out the whole curse thing but I told them the human truth. They deserved that much."

Alexei could imagine them: happy and loving, everything that Grey was. "What were they like?"

"She didn't have hardly anyone. All I found was a grandmother and a cousin. Her mom died ages ago and her father was never in her life." He sighed. "They asked about her body and I told them she was with our mother. I gave them the coordinates so that if they ever felt like it, they could see her grave."

"Thank you, brother."

"I'm glad you're alive, Alexei. It'll get better." Maksim wanted to say so much more but the words just wouldn't leave his tongue. He was crying on the other side of the phone but he'd never let his brother know; little did he know though Alexei was doing he same. "Please. Come live with me. The Rockies are beautiful, you'd love it."

"That's a place for a wolf, Maks, not me."

"You can still live here-"

"I can't leave her. It hurts too much."

Maksim was biting back sobs. "I love you, brother."

"I love you too." Alexei's head was buried between his knees. "Take care of yourself."

"You too."

And that was it.

Brother to brother. That was all they had to say, because they both knew deep down they were feeling the same things yet neither wanted to acknowledge it.

And as silence engulfed the mansion once again, with it came the cold fingers of a loneliness so deep Alexei could feel it in his bones. It made them ache as it's sinister fingers coiled around him and made him feel as if he was drowning. Drowning in his own tears and misery. He hated it, hated this weakness. It was a feeling he'd come to despise with every fiber of his being; it made him feel these human feelings that'd he'd never felt before and he hated it.

Although he knew he never could, and that everything that had happened was his fault, deep down he wanted to hate Grey. He wanted to blame this all on her because if she had never come here, he wouldn't be a human. If she had never found him in the trees that day, he'd still have a brother. If she never looked at him with those goddamn eyes, he'd still have a beast. And to him, being a beast was better than being a lonely human with no family or someone to love.

But he couldn't blame Grey, no matter how hard he tried. No matter how much alcohol filled his veins. No matter how much he cursed her name and trashed her old room. No matter how much he cried. He couldn't blame her. He couldn't even blame Petra. He couldn't blame anyone but his own self, because everything that happened that day was his fault. And he could still hear Petra's voice reminding him in his head, her voice driving him to insanity.